I0735625

Hellhound in a Handbag
An Obscure Magic Book 8

By

Viola Grace

Freddy was born to take the mantle of hellhound, but she wasn't fond of the idea. Wearing the responsibility to atone for the work of a homicidal ancestor, Freddy is the eleventh generation tied to the victim's family, and being bonded to a mage halfway around the world is tiring.

At a moment's notice, Freddy can be yanked from an event or her own bed and pulled across the world to act as the mage's familiar.

Her friends want to help, but there is only one way to get her out of the indentured servitude that her family has landed her in. She needs to find a stronger mage to take her on as a familiar. The hard part is finding a stable mage to link to. The weird part is watching her friends auditioning them.

Chapter One

Freddy lowered herself into the bubbles of her bath with a groan. Red and pink began to stain the water around her as she dropped into the tub.

Self-pity had gotten old by the time she was sixteen. Now, Freddy was just frustrated... and sore. Really, really sore.

"I am getting too old for this shit." She sank under the bubbles and let the heat work on her muscles. Being in her mid-twenties should be fun. She should feel energized and not exhausted, but the bitch in Europe liked to yank on their connection, and a fight normally ensued.

While she soaked, she pondered what

she had done to get tapped as her generation's familiar to the Nurfetti clan. The family name was now Smith, but the Nurfetti bloodline still laid claim to an indentured familiar. Bastards.

Freddy remained in the tub and looked at the marks on her arms and stomach that were already fading. Coming home covered in blood was not fun, but having to remove her clothing so that her rapid regeneration didn't fuse her to the fabric was a necessary chore.

The marks on her belly still showed the claws of the tiger that she had fought. Rolling over and over with it, she had stopped trying to bite and had used the claws on her hind legs to claw at it, forcing it to let go. A rapid reversal of position had had Mage Smith declared the winner with the stronger familiar, and she had collected her money. The moment that the fight was over, Freddy had resumed her normal familiar appearance, and the mage had scooped her up and dumped her into her purse. When they were clear of the fight, she was dismissed.

Sometimes, Freddy was pretty sure that the mage didn't realize that she was an actual person, but then, Mage Martha Smith didn't give a rat's ass. Freddy was portable when Martha wanted her in the purse and a hellhound outside of it. It hadn't taken the mage long to figure out how to get money from the use of her familiar.

Freddy didn't want to be a fight dog, but she had no choice. The moment she was summed, she lost her voice and her will. It was rough.

When her skin was healed, she soaped up her poof and set to work. It would be at least another twelve hours before she was summoned again. Her mage liked to sleep in.

It was a little counter-intuitive to get out of a bath, get dressed and then go dig in the dirt, but Freddy needed the serenity of her grandmother's garden with its variety of benign and predatory plants and inhabitants.

She was wrist deep in the bone meal for the sedation roses when her phone rang. "Yellow?"

"Hey, Freddy. Are you up for a late-night taco run?"

Freddy looked up and noted the moon overhead. "Sure. Meet you there?"

"We can come get you. We are in the neighbourhood." Benny chuckled. "We are actually in your driveway."

"I am in the garden. Be out in a minute."

She washed her hands in the nearby bucket of water, and then, she poured the contents carefully at the base of the flowers. The hints of red told her she hadn't been as careful with the roses as she should have been. Ah well, another creature in the world after her blood wasn't unexpected.

She shook her hands dry and walked across the grounds toward the small gate on the side. With a last longing look at her private oasis, she walked through the gate and was back in the world of lights, electronics, and magic.

The SUV was waiting in her drive with the familiar faces grinning at her until she got closer to them. A mass exodus from the vehicle made Freddy stop in her tracks.

Benny ran toward her, and there were tears in her eyes. "Geezus, Freddy."

Freddy noted the direction of their gazes, and she looked down at her arms. Now that the slashes were healed, bruising was covering her. Her face must be just as delightfully blue and scarlet. "Ah, sorry. I should have declined."

Agent Tremble came up to her and

gently lifted her arm. His lashes fluttered, and he scowled. "You were broken."

Freddy lifted her arm from his grasp. "I know. I was there. I was up against a very strong familiar."

Smith was frowning with concern, but he smiled slightly. "Not stronger then."

"No. I won the day."

Argyle shook his head. "For a mage, you are amazing at recovery."

Freddy sighed. "I have to be. It goes along with the link. Now, I believe I was promised tacos?"

Benny grinned and waved toward the SUV. "Hop in. We will discuss this on the way."

Freddy got in and sighed as Benny and Tremble went around to scoot in against her. She was locked in next to her best friend and her best friend's lovers. Not peculiar at all.

"Freddy, it is getting worse."

"You don't say."

Benny sighed. "I know that you aren't a fan of it either, but will you let me help you with this? I am sure that Minerva can find a spell or something."

"Minerva is wrapped up in her pregnancy. If she tried to make me a spell, it would likely rip me in two."

Argyle chuckled from the front seat, but no one else made a sound.

"Folks, I am recovering, and this is the longest time before another summoning. She is on the other side of the world and fast asleep right now." Freddy didn't mention that her mage was heavily into drugs and was going to have a short lifespan. As her familiar, the idiot was going to take Freddy with her when she went. It was a little fact of life that Freddy had come to terms with.

Benny made a face that stated baldly that she wasn't done talking about it. Freddy took her hand and gave it a squeeze.

They clung to each other for the rest of the ride to Taco Taco Taco. A little shared fire consumption would do wonders for her conversational skills.

She exhaled hard as she cleared her mouth and went in for a third bite.

"Wow, Freddy, you must be in rough shape." Benny shook her head and ate her own tacos covered in goblin-made chili sauce.

Freddy sighed as she swallowed again. "Yeah, when all my nerves are back online, this won't be nearly as palatable, but right now, it is amazing."

Argyle asked the question that the other two had to be wondering, "Why can't you ask to be reassigned?"

Freddy wrinkled her nose. "Because there was a loss of magic as well as loss of life involved. I am from a pure mage bloodline, and one of my ancestors had the nerve to win a duel of honour. The duel had been forbidden by the Mage Guild, so my ancestor was punished."

"But you were punished."

"Well, as the deceased's wife was pregnant, one of my ancestor's children was assigned as guardian and then familiar when the child was old enough. They were bound by the work of every arch mage and master mage that were in the country at the time."

Smith looked to Benny. "Is that a lot?"

Benny nodded. "Over ninety. They all threw their power into binding Freddy's family."

Freddy grimaced. "The deceased was an arch mage's son. They were making an example of my ancestor. He could tap into the demon zone for his magical energy, and it was considered an unfair fight, even though Smith had started the challenge."

Argyle nodded. "Right. Honour."

"Precisely. So, one member of my family has guarded one member of his for centuries. The eldest gets us as a familiar and chooses our shape. It is channelling us into an object of power and nothing more, but they were kind enough to give us our own time and life when we are not on duty. That was an innovation that began three hundred years ago when there was a sudden decrease in my family's population."

Benny blinked. "I didn't know about that."

Freddy shrugged. "I just learned about it when I was looking up ways to break the spell."

Benny stared. "*Is* there a way to break it?"

"No. It is rock solid for another three generations. Of course, since we are a straight line in our family now, that means that when I die, my line dies with me." Freddy sighed and sipped her soda before diving into her next taco.

"Freddy, what aren't you telling me?"

"Quite a lot. What are you looking for?"

"You have been fatalistic since before our bonding ceremony. What is up?"

Freddy looked around, among friends, and she blurted it out. "Given the way my mage hits drugs, booze, and unprotected sex, I will be dead in less than six months."

Benny's taco exploded in her fingers. "What?"

"My life is bound to hers. She lives the lifestyle she wants and uses my energy to heal herself. As these bruises show, I am running out of power. My hellhound had plenty of energy, but unless I am in that shape, I am subject to my body wearing out from the constant draw on me."

She kept eating while the others

looked at her in horror.

Benny blinked rapidly. "What can we do?"

"Nothing. I can't break the bond, the Mage Guild doesn't want to hear from me, there isn't anything to do. I am ready for it, and the curse will end with me unless my parents have more kids."

Tremble cocked his head. "Won't your father take up the mantle?"

"No, my grandfather died, and I was tapped for the next mage. There is never more than one hellhound at a time. It was part of the curse designed to keep my family going."

Tremble nodded. "So, it goes on to the next generation."

"Correct. If I managed to have kids, the child would be attached to the cousins or second cousins of my mage."

Tremble asked, "Not her children?"

"Oh, honey, that bitch isn't going to let kids wreck her body. She is doing that with the hard drugs." Freddy smiled and looked at her arm. The food was working. Her skin was resuming its normal olive tone.

She looked around at the others. "Quiet night?"

Benny smiled. "There has been a rash of recruiting at the XIA. We are getting ready for an out-of-city trip, so everything is being reported around us unless absolutely necessary."

Tremble chuckled. "Except for the mermaid hookers."

Benny snorted. "Except for that."

Freddy wiped her fingers. "I do have a plan."

Argyle smiled. "Do you?"

Benny scowled. "When did this plan emerge?"

"Just now. I am going to contact a few friends with contacts high in the Mage Guild and see what they think about my options. If anyone can find me a path, it is someone who is born to be lucky."

Benny blinked, and a slow smile crossed her lips. "I do like the way you think."

Freddy nodded. "It is the beginning of a plan."

The others nodded and then went to get the second round of food. Planning required fuel, and no one did tacos better than Dem-rah.

Chapter Two

reddy walked into the Spectral Consulting agency and headed into the office. She settled down and began working on the website that Imara needed to pull in business. It was time to start putting filters on the comment section. Folks were getting too keen on nocturnal adventure.

Imara rounded the corner with Mr. E perched in kitten form on her shoulder. "Good afternoon, Freddy."

Freddy smiled. "Good afternoon, Imara, Mr. E."

He leapt from his mage's shoulder to the desk and sat on the corner, making cute sounds. Freddy reached out to scratch his head and chin with a smile.

"Did you want some coffee?" Imara headed for the coffeemaker.

"Please." Freddy grinned and took a pen out of the pen holder on her desk to use it to taunt the ancient mage on her desk. Mr. E batted the plastic, and she laughed. Her mood was lighter in that moment than it had been since the night of the business warming.

Imara walked over with a cup with the swirl of cream visible as she set it down.

Freddy watched as Imara got her own cup and took a seat in the chair across from her. "So, Freddy, what can I do for you?"

Freddy was sipping her coffee. "What?"

"I can feel your question pressing on me. You are worried about something, and you want to ask me a question."

Mr. E hopped off the desk and wandered over to Imara, clawing his way up her jeans and over her top to settle on her shoulder.

"Does he know?" Freddy jerked her chin at Mr. E.

"He pointed it out."

Freddy sighed. "It is about my status as a familiar. I want to cut the ties to my mage."

Imara sipped at her coffee. "Right. What can I do to help?"

Freddy wrinkled her nose. "Help me find out how I can do it. I haven't been able to find a way out, and the Mage Guild won't help me."

Imara smiled. "Toss me the pad and the pen from the desk and tell me everything about the original documents. Give me two days, and I will meet you at Ritual Space for a brainstorming session."

"You are going to help?"

"Sure. My work is primarily in the

evenings, so I am all yours during daylight hours." Imara grinned. "I count you as a friend, and Mr. E understands about the lack of choice of mage that some familiars suffer. He lucked out."

Freddy watched as the kitten sat on her shoulder, grew into a full-sized cat, and let out a melodious yowl. From there, he jumped to the floor and became a man in mage robes. "We will help you, Fredericka. You might not gain a mage as forgiving and openhearted as Imara, but we will help you to cut off the cancer, somehow."

Freddy blinked. "I always forget you can do that."

He smiled. "It is part of the enchantment. When you need to remember, you will."

Imara wrinkled her nose. "He has a date with my mom tomorrow afternoon, or I would make arrangements for us to meet then."

Freddy blinked again until she thought that her lashes were clicking. "Right. Well, I have set up one of the automatic filters. The invitations to pornographic events should be minimized."

"Good. I had to look a lot of that stuff up. Now, when was the curse instituted?"

Freddy blinked as Imara got back to business. "Right. Well, here we go."

They went over details for three hours. Imara asked questions about family connections that Freddy had never considered. When she asked if any of Freddy's ancestors—who had the office of familiar—were spectres, Freddy had no idea.

"I don't know if our magic survives after death. It is mainly demon zone energy anyway."

Imara smiled. "That makes it easier. There are only two facilities that store that kind of spectre, and the nearest is only two hours away. I can make a few calls and find out if there are any of your people there, and if so, I want to speak with them."

"Do I need to come with you?" Freddy tensed. She could feel the pull on her magic from across the world.

"No, I can do this. I will see you in two days. Freddy?" Imara stood and reached out for her just as Freddy was pulled through the ether and into the presence of her mage.

Hopping around on stubby little legs was annoying, but being scooped up and stuffed into a purse that reeked of stale perfume and sweat was disgusting.

"There you are, Pinky. You delayed coming again, didn't you?" Martha scowled at her with darkly rimmed bloodshot eyes.

Freddy bounced and yipped lightly. It threw Martha's rage off and so carried

Freddy off toward the battle that she had picked. It was the same behaviour as her ancestor, but she used her familiar to carry it out, and there was money on the line.

Freddy looked out over the field and saw the giant Ferris wheel in the background. She stifled her groan. They were back in London.

She peered around the edge of the purse and noted the gathering of magic up ahead. This wasn't the normal setup of challenge and acceptance. Something was up.

She was going to have to put the situation into some semblance of sense because she and her mage didn't communicate. It was one of her favourite things about Martha. She talked to everyone but Freddy. Freddy was a utensil. She was due the same respect as a fork.

The scent of other familiars was heavy when they reached their destination. Freddy could smell the scent of animals and even one or two spectral projections. She didn't catch the scent of anyone like her, so she settled in to see what was happening.

Over a dozen mages were gathered with their familiars. When Freddy's mage arrived, a bubble expanded to encapsulate them all in a concealment spell. Duelling with familiars was against the law.

Freddy was the reigning champion. Her position as a penal familiar was a source of pride for her mage. It meant that she couldn't be sold or traded, so she was exclusively loyal by the curse that bound her.

When her mage took a seat to watch the battles, she pulled Freddy into her lap. A few folk snickered at the sight, but no one remembered what Freddy would become. It was the magic of the demon zone. It took a strong-willed mage to remember that the power had ever touched them.

Freddy sat on her mage's lap for an hour before someone had a winning familiar that they wanted to try against the champion. It was an eagle. Freddy hated eagles, the fight was over too soon.

When Martha sent her the command, Freddy got up, stretched and hopped down, trotting her tiny body into the centre of the arena, her nose twitching at the scent of blood laced with magic.

The crowd laughed at her. It was fine. They always laughed, until they screamed and tried to run through the barrier.

The eagle's mage threw it skyward. There was no time like the present. Freddy pulled power from the demon zone and took on her body as a hellhound.

It wasn't expanding her form; she wrapped the Chihuahua in demon energy, and she gained a barrier of magic that suspended her and removed physical limitations. She literally became the power from the demon zone, and that energy was limitless.

The eagle landed with its talons embedded in power, and it screamed as the shock ran through its veins.

Lazily, Freddy rolled to her back to knock the eagle loose, and when it was down—twitching—she picked it up in her mouth and carried it back to its mage. The human was doing its own share of shivering in pain, so being with its familiar was best for both of their recoveries.

With her opponent dispatched, she walked to the centre of the space, and she howled slowly, letting her energy return to the zone.

She trotted back to her mage and was scooped up and returned to the purse. From there, she was carried and then dismissed back home.

Freddy sighed. At least she didn't have any bruises or damage to explain. The slices and damage to her back from the talons were easy to deal with. At least she could reach it this time.

She got to her feet in her grandmother's garden. It was the spot she felt safest, and yet, it was still weird to get up from the ground, wearing the clothing and shoes she had had on earlier.

She found her phone and texted Imara that all was well. She was inside the house and headed to the shower by the time she got a response.

We are on for tomorrow. Put the time in your phone. See you at Ritual Space. Already have a few candidates lined up.

Freddy smiled as she peeled the bloody mess of her shirt from her back. For the first time in a long time, she was feeling upbeat after coming back. That one little text had done wonders for her mood.

Her shower started off with red, transitioned to pink, and finally, the water under her feet ran clear.

When she was clean, she wrapped one of her black towels around her and padded to her bedroom. Her parents' door was closed, as it always was when they were out of the country, and the careful padding of her feet made almost no sound in the empty house.

She spent a lot of time alone. When her job was done, there were only friends or silence. She really needed a hobby.

Chapter Three

$\mathcal{F}$reddy drove the forty-five minutes from her family home to Ritual Space. Her left arm was in a sling, but she managed to steer just fine for the short journey. It was with a heavy sigh that she parked in the lot and relaxed. This was when she found out what her friends had in mind for her.

The small door in the wall of fencing swung open, and Adrea was framed in the space.

"Come on in. This is going to be so weird." Adrea was grinning.

"What did you do?" Freddy walked toward her cautiously, her bound arm was tight against her.

"Oh, it wasn't me. Imara's familiar suggested this, and it is absolutely hilarious."

"Mr. E suggested it?"

Adrea led the way into Ritual Space, and the peculiar scene explained her uncharacteristic snickering. The master of Ritual Space had crafted a cross between an obstacle course and a medieval fair.

Imara was standing next to a tray of seeds, and her kitten was perched on her shoulder. Freddy wandered over to her.

"Imara? What is this?"

"Well, around that corner are twenty candidates—most are cousins on my mother's side, but I will explain that later—and they are going to be put through a series of tests and events... and so are you."

"Wait, so these are your relatives?" Freddy blinked.

"Most of them. It is part of the plan."

"What plan?" Freddy felt helpless.

"My plan. We are going to separate you from your mage, so we need a different one, and we have to abide by the original curse, so we needed members of the Smith family."

Freddy stared. "You are a member of that family." Her voice was flat. She could hear it.

"More or less. I prefer to believe I am in my own family and I invite people to join me."

Mr. E sat up on her shoulder, and he yowled proudly.

Freddy sighed. "Right. What kind of challenges are we engaging in?"

"Well, planting seeds. You can do it anywhere in the marked zones, but the positioning is up to you. It is an intuition challenge."

"Ah. Right. That is important."

"Correct. Now, if Adrea is ready, we can introduce you to the contestants who only know they have been granted a day in Ritual Space with the promise of something to take home.”

“Oh, wow. So, they don’t know why they are here.”

“Nope. We thought it was best. They all met the criteria that we discussed, and they match the stipulations of your curse, but beyond that, I didn’t fuss with it too much. You can talk with them, socialize with them, and make a few connections to narrow down the men for the next round.”

“So, this is a twisted game show.”

“No, this is a selection process that we don’t want to drag out. Adrea can keep you from being removed from this place, but once you leave the door, you are able to be pulled away. We want to delay that as long as we can.”

“You and me both.”

They walked into the maze of canopies and stalls manned by folk who were distinctly transparent.

Freddy blinked as they rounded the corner. Twenty men were standing or sitting around a large stone pit. Adrea clapped her hands, and all heads turned toward them.

"Gentlemen and lady, the Ritual Space has decided to let you plant something in its soil. The next half hour is for you to find the right seeds for you, and after you have chosen your five, you will wait until the others are ready, and then, as a unit, we will go out to determine who gets to plant where." Adrea smiled.

One man raised his hand. "Why is it a competition?"

She gave a slight nod. "Because Ritual Space does things its own way. If you wish to leave, a portal can be arranged."

He scowled and shook his head. "I don't have much use for plants, but this will be interesting to watch."

Freddy made note of him. He was willing to pipe up but still curious even if he didn't need the herbs.

Freddy wondered if everyone here was a mage, and when Imara smiled brightly at her from the sidelines where she had crept up, she guessed that they had to be.

Adrea answered the question that Freddy hadn't asked. "Now, as everyone here is a master mage, you can use spells and intuition to find the seeds that you need. You have thirty minutes to go through the stalls and select five seeds. You can trade them out with the vendors at the kiosk if you find one you want more, so choose carefully. Go."

Her softly spoken word was lost on everyone but Freddy. She turned on her heel and sprinted for the first kiosk she had seen. It was the one Imara had been leaning against, so that made it worth a look.

The thunder of feet behind her gradually faded as she reached the beginning. The spectre manning the booth smiled. "May I help you?"

"Yes, please. What are these seeds?"

"Apples."

"I would like one, please."

The spectre opened her hands, and Freddy cupped her fingers. A seed appeared in her palm. Oh, interesting. Manners mattered.

The seed turned gold against her skin.

The spectre smiled. "Would you like another?"

"No, this one is fine. Thank you very much."

"Enjoy the day." The spectre nodded. She was dressed in an outfit that would have placed her at the turn of the previous century, and she seemed to be delighting in the day out.

"You as well, madam. It is a lovely location."

The spectre beamed at her and faded out again, almost transparent and waiting for the next customer.

Freddy went along to the next station, and she looked the seeds over. She nodded politely to the male spectre in the kiosk and continued on.

The nasturtium seeds caught her attention next, and she waited patiently while two other contestants picked their seeds. When they had left, she greeted the spectral clerk and smiled. "Good afternoon, what are these, please?"

"Nasturtium seeds. Excellent companion plants for driving away pests." The man grinned.

"I would like one, please."

The seed appeared in her hand. She thanked the clerk and went on to the next three kiosks, getting a broccoli seed, a pumpkin seed, and a mystery seed.

When she was done, she returned to the centre where they had started, and she waited. Adrea sat down next to her and nodded. "Good choices. Plants for health, defense, and doing what is right."

"And a mystery seed and an apple seed."

Adrea bumped her slightly. "Who doesn't love a mystery, or apples for that matter?"

Freddy snorted. Across the way, three other men had come to have a seat in the open space.

Adrea got to her feet. "Well, time's up."

Freddy blinked. "Wait, what about the others?"

"Ah, they have been transferred to the outer edge of the property for their planting. Imara is supervising with Mr. E."

"And all the spectres."

Adrea shrugged. "Their families requested that they have a day out, so Imara obliged."

"That is amazing on such short notice."

"She is an amazing woman. As are you. Now, as for the other three with you. Let's go."

Adrea lifted her fingers and beckoned, and the three men jumped to their feet.

Freddy looked at the guys. There was a lithe but athletic redhead, a man with dark blonde hair and deep blue eyes, and the man who had spoken earlier with black hair and eyes that were a strange icy green.

Each of the men had one fist clenched around their seeds, and they followed Adrea where she led.

Freddy pattered along, and when she glanced back, the fantastical village was disappearing.

Adrea whispered grimly, "Never look back."

Freddy looked to the other men

around her, and they all blinked guiltily.

Adrea cackled. "Psych. Just kidding. You can look anywhere you want. The space is just being reclaimed."

They were walking deep into a forest, and the path was getting narrower. Freddy bumped into the blond, and the redhead bumped into her.

"Sorry."

Freddy paused, grabbed his hand and pried it away from her butt. "Apology accepted."

There was a growl from the burly brunette behind him. "Tessor, knock it off. This isn't one of your private jaunts."

"I just bumped into her. She isn't holding it against me, are you, pet?"

Freddy stopped in the centre of the small path, and she turned to the red-head. "I will never hold anything against you, and if you grab me again, you are going to feel my speciality, and I guarantee you won't survive it."

She stared at him and let the demon zone energy flow through her, just a bit. Adrea must have allowed it because the bright snapping green wrapped around Freddy like she was a holiday tree.

Tessor backed away stammering apologies. The seeds he had clenched in his left hand fell to the ground. The demon energy snapped toward them, but Adrea put out her hand and stopped it. The fire coiled in on itself.

"Ah, ah, ah. Reel it in, Freddy."

The gateway in her soul snapped shut, and the green flames stopped. Freddy blushed. "Sorry about that."

Adrea nodded. "Tessor, you are dismissed from this competition. Please return to the entryway where you will receive your parting gift."

Tessor looked around, and when he turned back the way he had come, a clear path opened in the woods, and he walked away with slumped shoulders.

Freddy felt bad but then remembered the weird caress that he had given to her ass. That wasn't appropriate, and she was right to do what she had, even if it meant flashing hellfire. Adrea knew what she was and hadn't freaked out, but she also waved the flames away, which was a bit surprising. Adrea wasn't famous for her defensive skills.

"Come along. It is time to get your focus back. You will need to concentrate on this if it is going to work." Adrea beckoned, and they continued on the path through the woods.

Freddy didn't know why she would need to concentrate, but the other two took the master of Ritual Space seriously.

The moment that they broke out of the thick walls of trees, the concentration requirement made sense. The ground had been churned up, and patches of dirt were ready and waiting in a weird polka-dot pattern across the meadow.

Adrea stood aside. "Choose one plot for each seed. If the ground accepts it, you will have all the fruit that that plant can offer."

The brunette murmured, "How do we know if the seed is accepted?"

"You will know." Adrea stepped back again, and she came close to melting into the trees.

Freddy looked at Adrea and had a hard time seeing her. She looked back at the men who were on either side of her, and she couldn't see them at all.

Freddy straightened her shoulders and looked at the field. When she couldn't decide, she opened her hand and whispered to her seeds, "Where do you want to go?"

She held her hand out toward the field, and as she swung it, her hand warmed up. "Right. That is very helpful." She strode off in the direction of the heat until her skin was nearly burning. She took the searing pain as a sign to stop.

Now, she just needed to figure out which seed wanted to be planted there.

How hard could that be?

Chapter Four

With her right hand, she dug the hole, and then, she held the seeds out over the vacancy. There were no volunteers. She looked around her and paused. The world had fogged over. There were only her presence and the earth under her knees.

Freddy smiled softly and picked up a seed with her soil-black fingers. She set it carefully in the hole and covered it with a soft pat. "Do what you can, little dude."

She got up and used her dowsing technique to find another spot to plant. Again, she knelt and placed the seed in the ground, covered it up, and whispered encouragement.

Freddy kept moving.

* * * *

Adrea watched the three move around the field. None of them could see the others. She was watching for a very specific behaviour, and when it began to emerge, she smiled. Two of the candidates were planting in the same mounds. That boded very well for compatibility.

It would be rude for Adrea to rub her hands together, but the inner chuckling was definitely appropriate. Blue was up near the gate, making sure that no one strayed into Ritual Space without permission. He was one determined bunny.

It seemed that Freddy's match was the handsome and serious Symon Smith. The plants would tell, but Adrea was fairly confident that she was right.

The ground under her feet was telling her that this was the way it should have been.

Symon Smith should have been Freddy's mage. He might have turned out different if he was, and that wasn't a good thing. He was a mage with strength and integrity. That strength may not have developed if he had access to the power that Freddy contained while he was young. Now that he was grown, it was the right time for him to blend his natural talents with hers.

Adrea sighed silently at the matriarchal position she had been wedged into. In some ways, she loved it; in others, it was a little hard to take when the folks she was mothering were older than she was.

When all of the seeds had been sewn, she raised her hands and removed the perception filter that she had placed over the trio.

* * * *

Freddy jumped in surprise when the fog lifted, and she was standing within two inches of the hulking brunette with the icy green eyes.

She stumbled on loose soil, and she blinked in surprise when she was caught with a hard arm around her back.

"Watch your step, miss. This place is full of holes."

She blinked and smiled slightly, realizing that he was holding her up with the light touch on her back. She straightened quickly. "Thank you."

"It was my honour. I loved your flame."

She stared at him and blushed. "Thanks. Family inheritance."

Adrea was standing ten feet in front of them, and the blond was a few metres to the right.

Adrea grinned. "Well, thank you all for your participation in this project. Please join me now and watch the progress."

Freddy stepped forward until she was next to her friend. The brunette settled next to her, looking out over the dotted landscape. The blond was on the other side of Adrea.

They all stared, and Adrea moved forward, her white hair ruffling in a light breeze. She lifted her hands out and whispered, "Thank you for your service, you may return to sleep now."

The open plots of land sealed up and green meadow covered them in under a minute. Oddly, there were only ten remaining dots of soil on the landscape.

"The rest of you can wake now." Adrea raised her hands upward, and for a moment nothing happened. The soil slowly shifted, and small tendrils crawled toward the light, pulling themselves out of the soil as their roots dove deep.

The apple seed that Freddy had picked wasn't growing alone. Another tree was rising with it, twining together until they burst into blooming branches.

She glanced at Adrea, but Adrea's focus was intense. The stranger next to her was looking beyond the apple trees, and when she saw what he was staring at, she jolted in shock.

Past the apple trees, along the furthest line of growing plants was something sprouting up from the base soil of Ritual Space that had no business being there.

Freddy took a step forward and then another. The brunette was at her side, and soon, they were standing together and looking at the creation that was about six inches tall and growing stronger by the second.

Her companion spoke softly, his voice

a smooth whisper of sound, "What is it?"

"It was my unknown seed. I am guessing it was yours as well."

The small twist of metal that was growing out of the soil was wreathed in fire. Demon fire. Specifically, Freddy's demon fire.

She crouched down and reached out to touch the flickering flame, but it was the metal that bent toward her fingers. The burn of the silvery coil was a surprise. It felt like her hellfire.

He knelt and reached out. The fire wrapped around his fingers, and he smiled. "It feels cold and hot at the same time."

She watched him play with it. "You have touched demon fire before?"

"There was an example at my master's forge. No one was allowed to touch it, but it called to me." He grimaced. "I had to change my path through the forge to avoid it."

"That is peculiar." She grinned. "I know most instructors would love to have demon fire on display and let their students play with it. That wouldn't get them into any trouble at all."

He chuckled and slowly pulled his fingers away from the flames. "You planted here?"

"I did. And everywhere you did as well. It seems we are going to have to split the proceeds." She smiled. "So, do you want the metal or the flame?"

Adrea's voice sounded behind them. "That belongs to Ritual Space. The other four can be split between you."

Freddy turned her head and saw the seriousness in her eyes. "So, this is just a tease?"

"No, it is an experiment to find you a possible replacement mage. You are compatible on a magical level; now, you have to explain to him what your situation is, and he will have to make a choice."

He got to his feet and looked down at Freddy. "What is she saying?"

Freddy got up and brushed her hands along her jeans. "Well, I think introductions are in order, and then, I will provide explanations."

Adrea called out. "There is tea set in the gardens."

Freddy nodded thanks and turned to her candidate. "Hello, my name is Freddy, and I am a hellhound bound to your family."

He paused and extended his hand to her. "My name is Symon, and I am a metal mage. What do you need from me?"

Freddy grinned and linked her arm with his, walking him out of the planting field and toward the gardens.

"How do you know your way around so well?"

"My friend got bonded here. We had

the rehearsal and the recon here. Also, I have been here for Imara's graduation celebration."

He blinked. "I got that invitation. I wasn't sure it was real."

Freddy snorted. "Imara is more than real; she's here with her familiar."

"Is she really the seventh child of a seventh child?"

"Oh, that. Yeah. I thought you were referring to the Death Keeper stuff."

He smiled slowly. "I thought that was an exaggeration."

"No. She can work with spectres, that isn't in doubt." Freddy looked around. The path to the gardens had taken a rather long turn.

"What do you do for an occupation?"

She wrinkled her nose. "I am currently between jobs, so I am keeping my family home up and running. I get free groceries and plenty of recovery time, so it works out."

"What happened to your previous job?"

"Ah, I ended up absent a few too many times. It is excusable at a regular office, but it sucks when you are supposed to be reporting on sporting events."

"May I ask what caused the absences?"

She wrinkled her nose. "This is the crux of the day, I guess. I am a familiar. I was born into a family curse, and when it was time, my mage called for me. My life has not been pleasant or predictable since."

He stopped, and she let him look her over. "You don't look like a familiar."

She snorted. "Is it the lack of fur and pointed ears?"

"Uh, yeah."

"Cursed familiars are different. It is a game that the Mage Guild likes to play with folks who have broken their rules.

One of my ancestors killed one of yours in a duel, and now, I am stuck with one of your distant cousins."

"What is the problem with your mage?"

Freddy let out a soft huff. "My mage is a brat who has been using me to intimidate her enemies and line her pockets. Even her own family hasn't been immune to her using me as a weapon."

He nodded, and they resumed walking. When he realized what she had said, he stopped again. "Weapon?"

"I am a hellhound. She used me to get her family to sign over wealth and properties. Currently, she uses me in familiar fights. It is agonizing and horrible to have to inflict such damage to other familiars. I hate it."

She flexed her fingers against his arm, and he placed his hand over hers. He was trying to calm her, and it was adorable.

"What happens when you return to your normal life?"

"I spend a few days recovering from the damage, and then, I try to get back to regular tasks. When the bruises fade, I go and have coffee with friends."

"Bruises?"

"Yeah, the slashes heal pretty early, but the bruises remain for quite a while. Some of the familiars I go up against have crushing strength and long fangs."

"Wait, she is forcing you to shift your shape and then fight other familiars?"

Freddy cocked her head. "I am fairly sure that she doesn't know I have a human shape. Her first summoning locked me into my default form, and when I fight, I become a hellhound."

"What would you do if you were free of her?"

Freddy sighed. "I think I would sleep for an entire day and know that I was safe, that I wouldn't be pulled away from friends or family. I would probably restart my life all over again."

"What if your new mage needed you?"

Freddy chuckled. "I would be there in a heartbeat. Literally. Though, a warning on my cell would be nice."

"What would you do for me?"

"Whatever needed doing. I can bring power and charm to any occasion." She smirked.

"I don't doubt that. So, I guess I just have one more question."

She led him to the tea set that was suddenly at the end of their path. Freddy sat down and poured tea for both of them.

She took one of the little sandwiches and smiled brightly at him. "What is your question?"

He took a tiny tea sandwich that looked ridiculously small in his grip. "What do I have to do?"

Freddy blinked. "You are serious?"

"I am. Do I have to kill her or something?"

"I don't believe so. The others are working on a transfer of power using your blood, and that of the original blood registered at the Mage Archive."

He sipped at his tea. "How long will that take?"

"Weeks? Days? Months? I don't know."

"And in the meanwhile, you are still being used by your mage."

"Yes, but if I can see the light at the end of the tunnel, things will be better."

"And you will be tortured."

Freddy smiled slightly. "I have already gotten today off, so things are looking up."

He stared at her with his icy green eyes. "You were summoned today?"

"I was, but no one can remove magic from Ritual Space, and that is what I become when I am summoned."

"When can we start this process? I will fight your mage if I have to."

Freddy nodded. "Good. You might have to. The good thing is that without my power, she hasn't got much skill. She uses a hammer to get through life, and I am her four-pound sledge."

He grimaced. "At least you are speaking of something I am familiar with. Who will be coordinating your emancipation?"

"Imara, her mother Mirrin, and Adrea. It isn't emancipation so much as transfer of attachment."

"So, how would you feel about attaching to me?" He raised one of his dark brows.

Freddy looked at his hand, and she smiled. "I would be delighted to be your familiar if you handed over that last cream puff."

He grinned and extended his hand. The bargain was struck.

Chapter Five

Freddy dreaded the ride home. Adrea had given her a bag with the fruits of the growing seeds, but it was just magical fruit and vegetables that would be applied to a later spell.

Symon got in his truck, nodded to her, and drove off with a wave. Freddy took careful steps away from Ritual Space until she was behind the wheel of her car.

Adrea was watching and waving from the doorway as Freddy pulled away from the parking area.

The pull on her magic went from a distant tugging to a hard yank.

The cool air of England wrapped

around her doggy form. Her mage hauled her out of the purse and shook her hard. "How dare you defy me, you little bitch?"

Freddy's small body was slammed into a wall, and then, she was kicked down a set of stairs, across a floor, and while she lay in agony, her mage scooped her up and dumped her back in the purse. "We have fights to win, bitch."

Freddy was bleeding, and it wasn't good. She tried to give the pain to her mage, but the woman wouldn't have any of it.

When they arrived at the fight club, and her mage set her on the ground, the room went quiet.

One of the others yelled, "What the hell is wrong with you? She's half dead."

Her mage nudged her with a foot. "She will fight, or she will die. Those are her options."

Freddy tried to pull her energy together, but she collapsed instead.

The blood coursing out of her mouth and nose made other members of the gathering look at her mage with shock and disgust.

"Fine. If you won't fight, get gone back to where you live."

Freddy was never so eager to get a dismissal in her life. She needed a healer in the worst way.

She woke up surrounded by white sheets and puffy pillows.

"It is about time that you were up, Freddy. I was beginning to worry. How did you get here?"

Freddy took a breath and smiled at how easy it was. She looked at Minerva in her queenly state of advanced pregnancy, and she inclined her head. "Thank you for your help. I needed a healer, and as you know, I am complicated."

Minerva snorted. "All cursed beings are."

"Well, thank you. I feel better. How long have I been here?"

"Three days. I have been in touch with Adrea, and she has had your vehicle returned to your family home. Benny is worried, and the Death Keeper, Imara, has something to keep a summons from happening again. She sent it along, actually."

"Sent it? With whom?"

Minerva grinned. "Her cat brought them. He was very polite, very charming, and he stayed to have a beer with my mate. That shit was weird."

Freddy was shocked into laughter, and she covered her mouth with one hand. The filigree band on her wrist was definitely new.

She looked, and her other wrist had the same flat and delicately woven band. She could barely feel it.

"There are two on your ankles as well. I must say, the workmanship is excellent. I have rarely seen such precise execution of the containment glyphs."

Freddy looked at them, and she traced the design with one fingertip. "Is there one around my neck?"

"Yes. Can't you feel it?"

"No. It is completely skin temperature." Freddy touched her neck and searched for the slight difference in texture that marked the super-thin metalwork.

"That's a good thing. If you don't know it is there, I can conceal it."

Freddy looked at them, and she cocked her head. "Can you get me the ingredients for an amulet or something? I can do the spell myself."

Minerva scowled. "Are you suggesting that I can't do a simple concealment spell?"

"I am suggesting that with all those

extra hormones in you, it might blow up in my face. I want both of us safe and sound."

Her pregnant friend exhaled slowly and picked up a notebook from next to the bed. "This is a simple one, so some herbs and a light enchantment should do the trick. You just need a focus object, and you are set."

Minerva's pen whipped across the paper, and when she was done, she lifted the page to her lips and blew on it. The paper stiffened, curled, and was a scroll worthy of an ancient mage in a few seconds.

"I love watching you do that."

Minerva smiled and got to her feet with a grunt. "I know. It's a kickass party trick. Now, I can send you home to your own bed."

Freddy looked at her friend and nodded. "Right."

"Well, my dragon will send you

through. We don't want you to end up halfway around the world."

"Thanks, Minerva. I really mean it."

"I know, Freddy. Take better care of yourself when you get your new mage. You deserve better."

Freddy blinked at the sincerity in Minerva's voice. "Thank you. I think that is the nicest thing you have ever said to me."

"I will get my fire-breathing idiot. Wait here." Minerva winked and left the room.

Freddy looked down at the parchment in her hands. The ingredients were simple, and the preparation was direct. The flicker of hellfire was the lynchpin, but it was an ingredient that she had in abundance.

Freddy got out of bed and snorted at the Grecian toga that she was wearing. Minerva was a fan of the classics.

Freddy looked around and located

her clothing and cell phone. She had just wrapped her hands around them when a pillar of light enveloped her. Apparently, she was going home right now.

Freddy blinked at Mirrin Deepford-Smythe and looked at Symon. "What am I doing here?"

"We are in the Mage Archives, and we are transferring your curse from your current mage to Symon." Imara walked into the small chamber and took her pile of clothing from her, setting it on a shelf against the wall.

"So fast?" Freddy was shocked at the timeline.

"Minerva and her mate had a conference with the guild, and they agreed that they wanted to live, and if your life was the price of that, they were handing you over to Symon."

Symon was looking her over with a strange expression in his ice-green eyes.

"I wasn't expecting you to look like this."

Freddy looked down and blushed. Slightly more humidity in the room and she would be naked. The muslin of her toga didn't hide anything.

Mirrin nodded. "They are waiting for us. If you are ready, Freddy?"

Imara snorted and picked up her familiar. She tucked him up on her shoulder, but he was busy staring at her mother. Imara murmured, "This is awkward. Mr. E, stop ogling my mother's legs. I know she is flashing all kinds of ankle, but this is neither the time, nor the place."

Freddy chuckled and fought the urge to cross her arms over her breasts. Symon had a definite interest in her curves that was both intriguing and terrifying. By the terms of the curse she was under, she couldn't say no to him once they were linked. The prospect was more appealing than it should be.

She walked with the other mages down the corridor and blinked in surprise at the three mages who were waiting for them.

Mirrin went up to them and handed the central figure a small box. Without a word, the man opened the box, nodded, and walked over to a small brazier in the corner of the room.

"Hold the familiar, please."

Imara gripped Freddy's left arm, and Symon grabbed her right. The mage whispered soft words, and he placed some of the contents of the box into the flames.

Freddy didn't have a chance to ask what was going on. The flames burned into her very soul. She arched her back and screamed as her magic and link to her mage were scorched. The fire of connection was something she had heard about, but not many familiars experienced it first hand and lived. Freddy wasn't sure she was going to survive it.

"Just hold on a few moments longer, Freddy. It is almost over, I promise." Symon's voice was urgent and caring at the same time. It was strange, as they didn't properly know each other yet. Freddy concentrated on his voice as he kept up the encouragement.

She was positive that her soul was nothing but ash, and sweat dripped into her eyes from the agony. A narrow-eyed glance at the mage in the corner let her know that he had opened a second vial and was pouring it over the embers in the brazier. The cool heat that washed over her was such a relief that she slumped into Symon's arms. Imara let her go and looked at her mother.

"The transfer of blood has been completed. Her previous mage has been removed, but the new mage of the same bloodline has been activated. Freddy is now bound to Symon's call."

The three mages filled out forms and had Mirrin sign them. As Symon was still supporting her, they brought the paperwork to him.

Freddy's voice cracked when she asked, "Just like that?"

Imara nodded. "Just like that. You only had to be beaten nearly to death before your soul and inherited magic was scorched to free it of the other family line. I am very happy that you survived, Freddy."

Mr. E stood up on his hind legs and pawed at the air while meowing.

"He is happy about your survival as well." Imara chuckled. "I think we should get you into your normal clothing. You sort of sweated that gown into transparency."

Freddy looked down and blushed. Yeah, she was the next thing to naked.

She tried to stand fully on her feet, but Symon was holding on. His green eyes narrowed as he looked her over. Finally, he set her upright and stepped back. "It is good to see that the bands fit."

Freddy blushed. "I am sure that that is what you were looking at. Is that it? Are we done here?"

Mirrin smiled. "We are. As a representative of the Smythe family, it was easy for me to sign the request. Apparently, you were to have been assigned to Symon, but Martha was born by C-section at the insistence of her mother ten minutes before Symon entered the world, making her the heir."

Freddy blinked. "What?"

"Oh, the services of your family are highly demanded. The entire family knows of the skills and power of the hellhound. I am surprised it doesn't happen more often, but once the birth has been registered, the line of succession to the familiar is set." Mirrin inclined her head.

Freddy's damp clothing was starting a shiver, and she nodded. "Okay, this is great. I am just going to get into my clothing, and then, we can continue the discussion before I pass out."

Imara nodded. "I will keep you company and watch the door. Mr. E, you stay with my mom. Keep all paws above the equator."

Mirrin gave a bright laugh and took the kitten, settling him on her shoulder.

Freddy sighed and headed back the way they had come.

Imara was true to her word and kept the doors guarded with fixed attention.

Freddy slipped her arms free of the top of the toga and pinned it in place with her elbows while she got her bra and shirt on. When the shirt hem was down around her hips, she grabbed her panties and wiggled into them. She didn't need to bother on Imara's account, but she had no idea who would come in through one of the doors.

Imara waited until she was zipping her jeans before she said, "I am sorry that it went so quickly, but you were in such horrible shape when you came back that I was afraid of what would happen if she could get her hands on you again."

"I know. It is all right. I feel surprisingly light if a bit sweaty." Freddy chuckled and put on her shoes.

"Symon's a good guy. I think he is a solid mage for you." Imara turned to face her. "He is the mage you should have had."

Freddy straightened and walked over to her young friend, giving her a hug. "Thank you."

Every bit of relief that she felt and the true gratitude running through her was in that hug.

"You are welcome. I wish I could have

helped earlier, but I didn't know anything about this stuff until this year, and I didn't meet you until recently."

Freddy laughed. "It is fine. I have learned what power can do, and I am wondering what intelligence can do as well. By the way, thanks for these bands, but I don't think I need them now."

Imara smiled. "Symon is insisting that you keep them. If he needs you, he will use a cell phone or a communication spell. No surprise summonses."

Freddy looked at the bands. "He did that?"

"He did. He can't call you now, but if his life depends on it, I am sure there is some kind of override."

"I will make sure of it. If he is my mage, my safety now depends on his. If I feel a tug, I will go to him."

"Excellent. I am fairly sure he is going to be low maintenance." Imara hugged her quickly. "Now, I have to get back to

Mr. E before he and my mother make a scene."

Freddy chuckled and folded the toga before draping it over her arm. "That is still an odd match."

"You don't have to tell me." Imara sighed and kept walking back to the ritual chamber.

Freddy saw Mirrin holding the kitten and scratching him under his chin. She stifled her snickers with excessive effort. It was exceptionally cute but a little weird. It followed the theme of the day.

Chapter Six

$\mathcal{F}$reddy had ten days to recover before she got the call.

"Hello?"

"Freddy? It's Symon. I hate to bother you, but I need a favour."

Freddy blinked. "Sure. What do you need?"

"Come to Seventeenth and Morkil. I need an assistant for a few days."

"When?"

"Now would be ideal, but as soon as you are able. Ask for me at the entryway, and someone will show you in."

Freddy blinked when the connection ceased. "Right. Seventeenth and Morkil. What the hell is at Seventeenth and

Morkil?"

She got up from her kneeling position in the garden and quickly changed into something that wasn't stained with dirt and chlorophyll.

The bands of silver on her wrists, ankles, and neck were already like part of her. They didn't give off any magical energy and were rather pretty. She had the concealment spell ready, but she hadn't used it. There was no reason to.

She got into her car and slid on her sunglasses. It was a bright day that was easing toward evening. She was heading due west, so a little eye protection was in order.

She left the city and headed toward the countryside. Seventeenth was a rural highway, and when she turned onto it and looked forward, she knew the location that she was looking for at first glance.

The dark tents looked a little odd under the bright sunlight, but the Night Faire was ready and waiting for the cover of night. That is when it would shine.

Freddy had no idea why Symon needed her help, but if it involved the Night Faire, she was all in.

She parked in the lot and got out of her car. The entry point was clearly marked, and there was a figure inside the security booth.

She walked up to the booth, and the figure moved swiftly to bar her path.

"We are not open to patrons yet."

She looked the man up and down. He was a goblin and troll blend. He could be out in the day, but it wasn't necessarily comfortable for him.

"I guessed as much. I am looking for Symon. He called and asked me to help for a few days."

The man smiled at her, showing a lot of teeth. "Ah, the new booth wench. Come with me."

Freddy had been called worse, so she followed the guard. The spell that they walked through across the gate made her grin. He hadn't needed to speak to her, the gate spell would have stopped her in her tracks.

She walked past booths that had their entryways covered with fabric, their signs advertised all sorts of bespelled items.

The Night Faire was whispered about as a place where anything was for sale. Magic or flesh, it didn't make a difference.

When he paused next to a booth, she looked at his back. "Are we here?"

He chuckled. "We are. If you are invited, you may draw back the curtain. I can't do it."

She sighed and stepped over to the slowly waving black fabric and pulled it to one side. The protection spell was strong, but she was able to duck under the fabric and stand inside the booth. Jewellery displays surrounded her. Every style and colour of draping, piercing, or other decorative use of metal were displayed in racks and on wooden heads.

"Symon?"

"Freddy? Wow, you made great time." He stepped out from the back of the booth, and she fought to keep her jaw from dropping.

Black leather covered his legs with faithful attention to every muscle and bulge. His torso was covered with a sleeveless leather tunic studded with silver. His eyes were the same pale green that she was getting used to, and his hair was confined in a thick ponytail that nearly reached the small of his back.

"Symon, how did your hair get so long?"

He blushed. "It is always this long. I just braid it and tuck it so that no one notices."

"Ah. That makes sense. So, what do you need me to do?"

He looked at her, cocked his head, and crossed his arms. "How attached are you to your dignity?"

"Not very."

"Do you have a problem being ogled?"

She grinned. "Nope."

"Excellent. Lo-rah is two booths down. She will set you up with clothing, and then, you can come back, and I will make you into a walking model for my work."

He shooed her out. "Two booths down on the right. Lo-rah is expecting you."

Freddy knew a dismissal when she heard one. She left his booth and went to the second on the right. She paused outside the flap and called out, "Lo-rah?"

"Come in, child. Let's see what I am working with."

Freddy pulled the scarlet panel aside and stepped into the booth. This one was full of fabric and leather. Some were occupying the same space.

The shadows in the space shifted and extended toward her. Freddy felt the power coming at her, and she straightened her shoulders to meet it head-on. The shadows wrapped around her, and she felt the careful contact. It was measuring her.

"You are a petite thing."

"Yes. That is a good description of me."

The woman's voice was low and rich. "Come into the shadows. My skin doesn't like the sun."

Expecting a vampire, Freddy was surprised to see a dark elf sitting at a table, hand sewing the edge of a hem.

Lo-rah had the charcoal skin and ashy hair of her kind, but her eyes were a startling blue.

"Hello, Freddy. I have your outfit here." She placed her hand on the pile of fabric next to her.

"Why do I need clothing?"

"We try to keep our clothing to that used five hundred years ago, in any part of the world. Your costume is pure fantasy, but also was the uniform of the vampire servants of the Costa Rican empire."

Freddy raised her brows. "So, I should be grateful this is summer?"

Lo-rah cackled. "Yes."

The fitting was fairly intimate but very quick. Lo-rah refitted the bra a few times until it gave the support and lift she was looking for. The skirt was billowing silk that hung straight unless she moved. When she took a step, the flare of the hem showed the slit that ran to the top of her left thigh.

Her belly, arms, back, and cleavage were all exposed. The bra was the same black silk as the skirt.

Lo-rah smiled. "Some soft boots and you are presentable."

The shadows moved into the shop area, and they returned with a set of soft black leather boots.

"They look authentic, but they have modern insoles. I am not a barbarian."

Freddy laughed and pulled her boots on. They were delightful. "Thank you for this."

"Don't thank me. I am charging Symon through the nose. Normally, I am still asleep right now."

Freddy chuckled and gathered the folded pile of her clothing. "Thanks for the help, regardless. This outfit is surprisingly comfortable."

"That is because you didn't get fussy about the lack of underwear. It is refreshing to work with someone who understands the line of a garment." Lo-rah smiled. "Now, you had better get back to him. The sun is setting, and folk are gathering at the gate."

She took the hint and scuttled with her normal clothing back to Symon's booth.

Once she was back in the booth, she looked around and headed to the back where he was looking at a series of chains and jewels.

"Where can I put my stuff?"

He waved off to the right, and she saw a locker with an open door. She closed it and pressed her finger to the lock. The click was audible.

"What next?"

She turned and faced him, keeping her hands at her sides.

He looked at her and heat flared in his icy eyes. "You look..."

"Like a booth wench. So, what comes next?"

He blinked rapidly, and then, he started the process of adorning her.

Hand flowers made all of her movements trackable, the wide collar of woven links draped down to tease the edge of her cleavage. An elaborate headpiece went on, draping down onto her forehead and keeping her hair in place, and the final wide belt with woven knots dangling settled around her hips at the edge of her skirt.

"Turn."

She spun, and everything settled into place. "I think it's all good."

He frowned as he looked at her. "Your ears aren't pierced."

"Nope. They were, but they heal every time I transform and then resume my human form. I got tired of having them re-pierced."

Symon nodded. "Understandable. No other piercings?"

"Nope. Same reason."

"Right. Well, I will have to figure out a few other accessories for tomorrow."

She smiled. "You really meant you need me for a few days."

"I do. My regular booth wench has had a new life opportunity and is making her mind up. Let me quickly walk you through the pricing system and explain my methods, and we can open the booth."

It was a quick explanation, and when she demonstrated competence with the sales equipment, he smiled and waved his hand. The front panel on the booth rolled up, torches lit, and they were open for business just as the sun set completely.

Freddy was front, centre, and on display. She took a deep breath, screwed a wry smile on her lips, and went to lounge in the doorway of the booth. If she was bait for her mage, she was going to be the best bait she could be.

She didn't smirk when she rang up

the ninth sale in two hours. Elves couldn't resist a human woman who appeared to be in a vulnerable position. A young human of sexual maturity was like catnip to them.

"There you are." She finished wrapping the necklace in waxed fabric that he was buying and turned to the elf with a smile.

He blinked slightly, and then, he gave her a slow smile. "Are you single?"

She could feel the push of a glamour against her mind. "I am, but I am not your type."

He held his parcel and frowned. "What do you mean?"

"You are seeking a subservient human female. I am decidedly not that."

He gave her a wry smile. "You could be."

"No. No, I couldn't." She looked at him and let her eyes shift to red.

His eyes widened in surprise, and his

smile became genuine. "You are right. You are not what I am looking for."

She grinned. "Please, frequent our establishment again." She folded her hands in front of her and gave him a polite and subservient bow.

"You can't blame me for wishing."

"I don't blame you for anything, but I am what I am." She straightened.

He inclined his head, took one of her hands, and pressed a kiss to the chain on her knuckles. "Another day."

She smiled and nodded. He left the booth with a spring in his step and a determined set to his shoulders.

She adjusted the folds of her skirt and turned back to tidy up the pay stand.

"You are very good at that."

She glanced over and smiled at Symon. He was a little sweaty, and a tendril of hair was falling over his left eye.

"What are you talking about?" She knew what he was referring to but wanted to hear him say it.

"You are excellent at turning men down."

She shrugged. "I prefer to be the one in pursuit. When guys come after me, I know it is because I look like a target."

Symon cocked his head. "Is that how you see it?"

"If they are after me on the basis of a first impression... yes."

His stare was astonished.

"Sorry. I know that genetics is no in-dication of character, but if that or my senses are any good, I know that I am after something specific."

"What is that?"

She smiled and gave him a slow look up and down before she whispered, "Trust."

He took a step toward her. "Just that?"

"It is what I have not been able to give or get in my relationships. It is what I value the most." She took a step toward him. "Now, I have one question."

He moved toward her, and she could see his intense focus on her in every line of his body. "Ask it?"

She made her voice husky as she leaned toward him. "When do I get a break? I am hungry."

Symon paused and let out a short bark of laughter. "Go. Charge anything you like to the booth. I will settle up with them."

She didn't need to be told twice; she turned, and her skirt flared wide. With long strides, she headed out into the Night Faire. This was a dream come true. For the first time in her life, she wasn't fearing a summons from the psycho she had been tied to.

It was time to locate some fun.

Chapter Seven

The moment she left the booth, sounds and smells rushed in on her. The spells that insured privacy and a pleasant shopping experience kept the Faire from encroaching into the booth.

The wind ruffled her skirt as she walked through the throngs of extranatural beings. The number of humans was miniscule, and all of those were mages. No unpowered human could even find the Night Faire.

Music suddenly wrapped around her and pulled her in a direct line from the booth toward a large open area being used as a display space where elves and goblins were dancing in formal measures for the folk watching. Freddy knew those dances. She and Benny used to go out together to the karaoke clubs, and Benny would growl, gargle, and belt out goblin torch song after song. Freddy would dance.

Part of her original teenage self was called by that music, and she wanted to dance.

She moved to the edge of the crowd and swayed with the music. A dark elf caught her gaze, and he smiled, walking toward her and bowing low. He extended his hand, and the invitation was clear.

Life had been too short so far, so she didn't hesitate. On the next measure, she joined the dance.

Her mind went blank, and her body moved in time to her partner, spinning, whirling, and leaping with the pulse of the music and the soaring of her soul.

This was fun, and she had found it.

* * * *

"Symon, you have to see the newbie." Hector growled it from the doorway to his office.

Symon looked up from the staggering amount of receipts that Freddy had taken in for very exotic and expensive items. "What?"

"Your new booth wench can dance." Hector waggled his brows.

"She's dancing?" Symon frowned at the half-elf-troll mix.

"She is more than dancing, the tips are flowing in. She is making them more money tonight than they made all last week. They might want to keep her."

Symon scowled at the leather-worker and left his booth, activating the protections as he passed the doorway. The music was hard to ignore, and the fast pace of it quickened Symon's steps. He was looking forward to seeing Freddy in action. He didn't have to wait long.

Freddy was dancing with Mosk if dancing could be considered the word. She was holding his arm as he swung her around, and it appeared that she was flying.

Her left leg was exposed to the top of the thigh, and her right was shrouded by fluttering fabric. As she was brought down to earth, her feet touched, and she pivoted in Mosk's embrace, bending back until her hair swept the floor.

The music ended with a surge, and the applause was deafening. Symon added his clapping to the throng, and soon, there was a surge to put money in the tip box at the edge of the slightly raised stage.

Freddy was sweating, the silk of her clothing was sticking to her with devastating faithfulness. Symon shivered slightly at the image in front of him, and she looked around at the audience and gave him a blinding smile when she saw him. His heart flipped in his chest. Was he supposed to feel this way about his familiar?

* * * *

Freddy turned to leave the stage, and Mosk gripped her hand. His smile was beguiling. "Another dance?"

"No. I have to get back to work. I was supposed to have been finding food, but I can make it the rest of the night without a snack. Thanks for the dance. It reminded me of fun." She winked at him and left him.

Symon was in the audience, and he offered her his arm. The elves were staring, so she took his arm and tucked herself against him. "Thank you for the retrieval. They have a glamour in their music, and I didn't want to fight it."

"You are an amazing dancer."

She grinned. "I have had a lot of practice."

"Really?"

"Yeah, my friend has some siren genes, so she likes to sing karaoke, and I like to dance. Since we hang out at the extranatural joints, I dance with a lot of extranaturals, with all of their tradition-al variations."

He nodded. "That is interesting. Is your friend extranatural?"

"Yup. She is so mixed that she usually looks human."

"Usually?"

Freddy grinned. "A girl likes to get changed for special occasions. Seriously, she is in the XIA. Their first official mage on a team."

"I thought you said she was extranatural."

"She is, but both of her parents are high-ranking and devastatingly skilled mages, so she got a lot of homeschooling."

They were back at the booth, and she could feel folk from the dance display following them.

Symon glanced over his shoulder. "I wonder what they want?"

"Perhaps to purchase some of your silver wares. The drape of the chains on my hip did stop me from shaming my ancestors. Thanks for that."

He blinked and chuckled as they entered the booth, and he removed the security block from the entry point.

Freddy sighed that the informal chat was over. Back to work.

The next two hours were spent speaking with women who had admired her accessories while she danced, and they wanted versions for themselves.

Freddy didn't know if she wanted to be held up as a model of style. She certainly didn't want to be in the spank bank of the male companions of all those ladies. *Ah, well.*

Every extranatural was met with a smile and politeness. Each face reminded her of friends growing up. It was incredibly relaxing to be with trolls and not mages for a change.

A gong rang in the depths of the Faire, and she quickly rang up and wrapped all the purchases for the customers lining up. They grinned, thanked her and left the booth rapidly.

When the final parcel was handed over in the waxed cloth, she sighed and tidied her station.

Symon emerged from his workshop and looked around. "Where is everything?"

"Sold. I have a stack of custom order requests over here. You can go through them and see if there is anything you would like to do." She smiled brightly.

He blinked slowly. "How?"

Freddy shrugged. "Cursed familiars transfer their luck to their mages. My mother was lucky, and so I have more luck than most. Will you be able to keep up with sales?"

He gave her an astonished look. "I have a lot of finished pieces that I keep in storage during the offseason."

"Bring the most expensive ones here, and I will get rid of them for you. How long am I working with you?"

Symon rubbed the back of his neck. "My previous assistant quit to go and open her own booth at a nearby human Faire. She told fortunes."

"I can see that the honour of being a booth wench might be lost on some people." Freddy leaned against the counter while he flicked through the custom orders. "So, what was that gong?"

"One hour to sunrise. The patrons like to be safe indoors before the sun burns them."

"Right. Makes sense." She wrinkled her nose. "So, where do I put all this hardware?"

He glanced at her and closed the booth to any last-minute customers. "To the workshop."

She followed him to the workshop and stood still while he removed her necklace.

"I noticed when you danced that this flipped a little. I will pick out something more suitable tomorrow."

He removed the belt around her hips, and the move was oddly intimate. He put the belt on a mannequin and set her headpiece on a wooden head. The last things to come off were the hand flowers. The chains, rings, and bracelets were her favourite part of the outfit.

"I am sorry to be parting with those."

He grinned. "I can have something similar if not exactly this set for you tomorrow. It is the least I can do."

"The least you can do is nothing. This reciprocal attitude is something I am not used to."

He blinked. "Ah. Right. Well, as long as you are my familiar, I will be giving at least a token for your services."

"Excellent." She rubbed her hands together.

Symon chuckled. "You did extremely well today. Thanks for coming when I called."

"It was my pleasure. It was also a compulsion, but it was my pleasure." She winked. "Now, how do I get my clothes back?"

He sighed, "Your locker will open at your touch."

"I know. Where is it again?"

He walked over to the lockers and bent down, pointing at the locker where he had placed her clothing.

She enjoyed the view until he straightened. He had a world-class ass.

"Right. I will just get dressed in my mundanes, and then, I will be on my way. Do you want me here before sunset again?"

"Yes. I will have everything in place. Um..."

"Yes?"

"Would you like to go for breakfast?"

Freddy grinned. "As soon as I have panties on, I am all yours."

He laughed and left the area, casting one comment over his shoulder. "Story of my life."

She was still smiling when she finished getting dressed and had her new clothing draped over one arm. It definitely needed a drip-dry. Dancing made her all sweaty.

Chapter Eight

She met him at a local pancake restaurant that was humming with folk from the Night Faire. It was a chance for the vendors to have some time to themselves.

The serving staff of the restaurant had determined expressions on their faces. They were going to be efficient and pleasant if it killed them. There were exorbitant tips that hung in the balance.

"So, is this tradition?" She unrolled her cutlery with a flourish.

"More or less. Since we work the Faire, it is our only chance to meet and talk shop." He shrugged.

"How long have you been doing this?"

"Well, I have had a booth since I turned nineteen. The metalwork mixed with my magic on an elemental basis, and there is a market for it in the extranatural world. Mage magic can't be exercised by them, but it can be triggered."

"Right." She nodded. "So, I noticed that most of the chains held perception enhancers."

"They are the most popular. I also make chains for protection, seduction, and arousal."

Freddy was stunned. "Really?"

"Sure. There are many folk around who have dysfunction issues. It isn't simply a standard human or mage concern."

"Wait, so what was the enchantment on what I was wearing?"

"Natural beauty. No matter what you have for characteristics, the magic enhanced them in the most flattering light.”

She smirked. “So, it wasn't my dancing that got the attention.”

“Oh, the dancing was all you. It was amazing, and it makes my stiff efforts look pathetic.”

Freddy shook her head. “I haven't seen you dance, but I am guessing that you are just fine. It is the lack of practice with a capable partner that makes folks insecure.”

“I see. Are you willing to instruct me?”

She grinned. “Of course. Name the place.”

His pale green eyes lit with amusement. “You are serious?”

“Of course. If it is a concern, you won't get better without practice, and as I am between jobs right now, this is the perfect time.”

He raised his brows. “You do have a

job. You are my booth wench for the week."

She was about to take umbrage when her plates arrived. Bacon, eggs, hash browns, and a double stack of pancakes.

"Wow, you don't believe in small portions, do you?" Symon looked at her selections with surprise.

"I haven't eaten for several hours. Being charming takes a toll on me." She poured syrup on all the essentials and smiled brightly at the server as the woman placed her toast down in front of her. "Thank you."

The woman smiled and drifted away.

Symon picked up his hamburger and started in on it. Freddy didn't hesitate, she began to plow through her meal like it was her last.

In between bites, she murmured, "If I think about it, I last ate about twenty-two hours ago. No wonder I am hungry."

Symon's features showed remorse. "I

should have given you more warning."

"Not necessary. I am used to being summoned out of every situation you can imagine. I only made it to my best friend's bonding ceremony because it was held at Ritual Space."

"Did that make a difference?"

"The only magic at Ritual Space is the magic that Adrea allows."

"Is she really that powerful?"

"You saw her in action. She can ask the land to do what she wills, and it will usually agree."

He smiled. "How did you meet her?"

"Through my friend Benny. Before that, I met her predecessor. She would have the Mage Guides over for sleepovers. It was weird but fun. You could feel the magic around you."

"So, you trained as a mage?"

"Trained and graduated. I don't have master status, but I get by." She waved a piece of bacon in the air like a magic wand.

"Somehow, that surprises me."

"It is the familiar thing, right? I try not to let it define my life. So, I majored in journalism with a minor in magic."

"You live with your parents?"

Freddy wrinkled her nose. "Not really. They travel, and I keep the house up. Same for my grandmother's place. I garden and tend the grass. It keeps me off the streets."

"With your life more stable, will you seek out another job?"

"Sure. As soon as I finish with your evening needs. Wait, that sounds wrong. As soon as you no longer have need of me."

"I am thinking that I will always have need of you in one way or another and that thought is unsettling."

Freddy was surprised. He seemed genuinely shocked that there was a bond between them.

"It is simply the familiar-mage bond. In the opposite sex, it produces attraction. Sometimes in the same sex as well, but generally, it also can create a sibling bond if the two are connected at a young enough age."

"We were not connected young."

She smiled. "No, we were not. We will have to be stuck with attraction or get comfortable enough to act on it."

He gave her an unfathomable look and continued eating his burger and fries.

When she was done, she sat back and fished out her wallet, reaching for cash.

He held up his hand. "After all you have been through, my treat. Please."

She inclined her head gratefully and looked around. To her shock, Mosk walked up to their table and looked to Symon. "We need her."

Symon cocked his head. "I need her as well. My needs win."

"We will trade you for Vishani. She loves working in your stall."

"No, I am afraid that Freddy remains with me."

Freddy felt it necessary to step in as the elf was just tightening his shoulders and lower jaw for the negotiation.

"I am not going to be traded. I might be persuaded to dance once or twice an evening, but I will need compensation for it in the form of food, and someone has to take my place in Symon's booth while I dance. He will not suffer because the troupe needs a human-looking dancer."

Mosk blinked. "You two are bonded?"

Freddy reached out and took Symon's calloused hand. "We are. Newly bonded, not yet mated. It is a delicate time to be swirling around in another male's arms."

That seemed to get through to him. "Ah, I understand that delicate time.

Four dances?"

"Two, and don't forget to feed me." She glared at him.

"Done." He extended his hand, and she took it, sealing the bargain.

Symon also agreed, and soon, there was celebrating at the table where the dancers were talking shop.

Symon shook his head. "I would have refused. You are not something to be loaned out."

"I know, but I enjoy the dancing, and I haven't been able to feel free for years. The combination of being at the Night Faire and the dancing has made for a lovely evening."

"The Faire is open for another six days in total. Will you come each of those days, rain or shine?"

"Of course. Do you attend other Faires around the country?"

"No. This is my one and only. I spend the winter stocking up and developing new patterns.”

“Nice. Do you have family?”

“Two younger brothers. Tons of cousins.”

She nodded. “I am an only child. I was, also, not planned. The family curse forced me into the world.”

“Are you serious?”

“Yup. The magic forced me through three kinds of birth control.”

“Three?”

Freddy ticked them off on her finger. “Condom, the pill, and separate bedrooms. Once she was pregnant, nothing could dislodge me. Apparently, they tried.”

Symon gave her a sober look. “Doesn’t that upset you?”

She sighed. “They were trying to save me from the servitude to an unknown mage. Only magic kept me alive on several occasions. I was pulled from friends, family, and my home without warning. I was chewed up and spat out, coming home bloody and broken. It has been agony, but my friends have remained there for me the entire time. Even my family came around and offered what support they could. It has been mainly financial in nature, but it still helps."

"How did you meet your friends?"

She laughed. "Benny was at my school. We ended up in the Mage Guides together. The others were collected along the way."

He nodded. "So, if you hadn't been under the curse of being attached to a mage, what would you have done?"

"I have no idea. It was never an option. I simply was born into this position, and I have to live with it." Freddy daintily wiped her mouth and pushed the empty plate stack aside.

"Would you ever have children?"

Freddy blinked. "Huh. You know, no

one has ever asked me that before."

She sat back and looked at him as she thought about her answer. "My child wouldn't be the cursed one, but their child would be if I were already gone. It is assigned to the next available child when the current familiar dies. As I am planning to make it into my sixties right now, I don't know if I would like to pass the curse down."

"What if we could lift the curse?"

Freddy felt tears prick her eyes. "We have tried. The Mage Guild won't hear of it. This is our curse, and we have to run it out."

"How many more generations?"

"They won't tell us. We are the penitent. We don't have a right to know, and since we have been stuck in our familiar shapes by our mages, we haven't been able to get them to ask. Not that they would."

"I will. I will ask and look into what it

will take to set you free.”

She didn't want to cry, she tried to hold it in, but a single tear ran down her cheek. “Thank you. Any little bit will help.”

“I aim to do more than a little.”

Freddy smiled brightly as the server brought the bill and he took it. He set out the cash, including a nice tip, and got to his feet. He extended his hand to her, and they walked to the door.

When they reached her car, he leaned down and kissed her on the cheek. “Drive safely. See you in fourteen hours.”

She smiled. “I will be there.”

He waited until she was driving away in the pale light of dawn, and the last thing she saw was him getting to his own vehicle. With a bizarrely light heart, she drove home. The gardens were going to get a tending to before she slept.

Chapter Nine

Freddy had never been happier to get to work. When she bothered to check her phone, Benny had been blowing it up with texts.

Explaining that she was a booth wench by night had caused a demand for details, and once Freddy had explained where and when she would be at the Night Faire, she knew to expect a visitor, or four. Tonight, there was going to be an XIA invasion.

She cleared the entryway with only a slight tingle of magic and a nod to the guard in the shadows. The route to the booth was simple, and she ducked under the drape before heading back to the workshop.

"Good evening, Symon."

He looked up from his workbench and then looked down again. "Good evening, Freddy. I am almost done here."

He was holding his hands out about a foot apart, and in the gap between them, a writhing mass of silver twisted and turned around a brilliant red gem. Fire wrapped around everything, sending a glow against his features that cast him in a semi-demonic light.

She watched closely as the metal licked at the stone, settling into a surround that continued to grow until the detailed span on either side of the stone was two inches wide and curved into an arc.

"What is it?"

He grinned and picked up a chain, linking it to the edge of one side and then mimicking the move on the other.

"There. You now have a proper headpiece."

She blinked. "Seriously? That's for me?"

He walked over to her and settled it in place. "Yes, it is for you. It will also record anything that causes an adrenal reaction in the fear range. If you are scared, I will know."

She blinked and touched the warm metal. "That is my job."

"Consider this a reciprocal arrangement."

Freddy scowled. "I don't need to be protected."

Symon raised his eyebrows. "Then, consider this an order. When you are at the Faire, wear the headpiece."

She grimaced. "Right. Let me just get into my outfit, and I will be ready for whatever happens next."

"There are new clothes for you. Lorah was watching you dance, and she thinks she can do better, so you are wearing her experimental designs now as well."

Freddy sighed. "Right. Fine. Can I get some privacy?"

"Of course."

She looked around and saw the soft crimson skirt and top that had been set aside for her. It would match the headpiece, and that was something.

When she had it on, the skirt was one and a half circles of the soft fabric. Each half circle was only sewn a few inches down over her hips, the rest was an embroidered seam. As she twirled, the embroidery was exposed, but when she stood still, the patterns were hidden. The top was a deeply cut choli that had the same patterns around the exposed edges. It acted as bra and shirt while leaving her back nearly naked.

Freddy locked up her clothing and cell phone before walking back into the main area of the workshop. "Symon?"

He walked in from around the corner. His admiration was burning in his gaze again. "You look..."

"I know. Lo-rah knows just how to cut a skirt." She gave him the out of the comment.

"You look stunning. It always surprises me that a woman like you doesn't have a man in her life."

She wrinkled her nose. "I have had several. I just scare them all off."

He shook his head as if waking from a trance. "Right. Now for today's costume."

She stood with her hands out and away from her sides as he wrapped her waist in a belt that pinned the skirt to her hips. Today's offering was studded with matching ruby jewels and had dangling links that held the skirt to her thighs.

"I am sensing a theme here."

"Your skirt yesterday nearly gave me heart failure. This will keep it covering everything." Symon smiled.

She giggled as he set the hand flowers into position.

"I am sensing another theme." She wiggled her fingers, and the ruby gems glittered.

"Your eyes glow red when irritated. It happens a lot, but it gave me the idea for this. I have had the gems around for ages, and this was a fun project."

"Wait, you did this all today?"

He grinned. "I was inspired."

She sighed and touched her chest. "No necklace?"

"Not quite. I kept your mobility in mind, so I kept things light." He turned and opened a chest, lifting out a glittering clash of chain and rubies. He walked around behind her and fastened the choker and collar around her, settling it so that it rested across the top of her breasts and over her shoulders.

The cool rustle of chain was a little distracting on her bare back, but she was guessing that was the point.

She lifted her hand and slowly pivoted in place. He was right. She wasn't weighed down by what she was wearing. "Well done, Symon."

"I am still working on ear adornment, but I haven't quite figured it out yet." He looked her over and nodded. "You look booth appropriate."

She cackled and wiggled her toes in the new boots. "What age are we supposed to be mimicking?"

"The golden age of the wave, when elves were around every hillock and mages cared for their devoted servants." He quirked his lips in a smile.

She snorted. "Right. Since I am early today, can I go and take a look around?"

"Of course, just be back when the gates open."

She bowed low. "Yes, my mage."

He didn't reply, so she skipped out and went exploring.

She had made it to the fifth booth that had opened its flap when one of the leather workers asked, "Are you Symon's wench?"

Freddy cocked her head. "I am."

The man was huge, and he stepped forward to extend his hand. "I am Hector, a friend of Symon's. You are quite light on your feet."

She took his hand and blinked as he raised it to his lips. "Uh, thanks. It is just a misspent youth and a lot of practice."

He chuckled and released her hand. She pulled her fingers back slowly. He looked like an elf that did steroids, but the protrusions of teeth on his lower jaw said troll.

She finished her introduction. "I am Freddy, by the way."

"Will you dance again?"

"Of course. I struck a deal with Mosk last night. I dance twice, and he buys my food for the night."

"Symon went for that?"

"Sure. He gets a booth wench while I dance, and I get my fee in food."

Hector smiled. It showed an unsettling amount of teeth. "How are you enjoying the boots?"

She lifted the edge of her skirt, and her boots peeped out. "They are very comfortable."

"Good. When Lo-rah asked me for a rush job with the silver and crimson colour scheme, I wasn't sure that I could get it done. I am glad I did. You look splendid."

She grinned. "I am glad that Symon has such charming friends. I had better get back. The gate is about to open." She jerked her head toward the red sky.

"I will see you later, Mistress Freddy.

I hope you have a profitable experience at the Night Faire."

She curtsied and headed back to the jeweller's booth. She waved at a few of the dancers who were making their way to the stage, and to her pleased surprise, they grinned and waved back.

Symon was waiting in the doorway to his booth, and he grinned as she returned. "Have a nice tour?"

"Yeah, give me a few more days, and I might make it to the end of the row."

He snorted. "There is a lot to see."

"There is. Now, what do you do in the back while I am in the front of the house?"

"I work to replace the stock that you are selling. I can do it at the smaller workbench if you would like the company."

She smiled. "Only if it won't disturb your concentration."

"I will try and see how it goes."

It was a start, and before she could turn around, the energy from the incoming crowd was pressing toward them. It was time to be the best wench she could be... again.

She could see Symon watching her out of the corner of her eye as she sold six bracelets for self-control to a goblin about to go into her first heat. She wanted to make the right choice and control was important. She couldn't be led by her impulses and commit too early.

Freddy wrapped up the bracelets after she finished the transaction. She handed them over with a smile. "Use these whenever you are afraid of your lust getting out of control. They won't stop it, but they will keep your head clear."

The young goblin smiled with her shark-like teeth and bobbed her head in thanks as she took her precious parcel and left the shop.

There was a lull in the activity, so she turned to Symon. "Are you working or ogling?"

He shrugged. "Both?"

She snorted and looked to the moon. She lost her concentration for a moment, and then, she shook herself and looked over at Symon.

"Freddy, are you all right?"

She blinked, and the haze left her brain. "Yeah. I think I just got a little focused on the moon. I will be fine."

"Do you need to rest, drink, eat?"

She laughed. "No. I am fine."

Benny's voice came from behind her. "I should hope so. Freddy, that is a killer outfit."

Freddy turned and looked at Benny watching her friend's expression change from friendly to wary. "What?"

"Your eyes, Freddy. You are leaking hellfire."

Freddy turned and looked at the polished steel next to the cash register. The mirror showed her green flames leaking out around crimson eyes. "Oh, dear."

Benny came up to her and whispered, "When did you last use the fire?"

"Um, the day I came home from that summons. These bands restrict the power."

Benny looked to Symon. "Can she take them off?"

"I will do it." Symon removed the elaborate necklace and the hand flowers in a few seconds. The collar that he had made came away at his touch, as did the bracelets.

"That should be enough. You can access your power now, just not change your shape."

She nodded, and the urgency to blow off some hellfire was immediate. "Where?"

Symon threw a ward around his booth. "Here."

She didn't need to be told twice. With a deep breath, she raised her arms above her head and let the fire burn free.

* * * *

Symon watched the woman he was falling for projecting hellfire skyward. It hit the stratosphere and splashed outward, and still, it kept coming.

Her friends were standing at a safe distance and watching her. He didn't know what he was expecting, but seeing the XIA uniforms and the stern menagerie of men standing behind their female, he was surprised. "You were a Mage Guide?"

Benny chuckled. "She has shared that, has she? Yes. We studied magic at my family home while she tried to keep up with her looming curse."

Symon glanced back at Freddy, and she continued to burn through the demon fire. He walked up to her, and he put his hand on her shoulder. The flames licked around his hand and crept up his shoulder.

"Freddy, you can stop now."

She closed her fists, and the flames shut off. She shivered and looked at him with tired but human eyes. "I think that took care of it."

One of the XIA agents made a call and reported that the situation was under control. When Symon heard through the phone that the light was being reported for miles, he sighed.

"Freddy, did you have any idea that you were building up that much power?"

She shook her head and reached for the cuffs to connect them again. "No. I didn't feel anything until the floodgate opened."

Benny cleared her throat. "I think I can explain."

Symon looked to her. "Please. Tell me

what you can."

* * * *

Freddy was tired, but she felt better after purging the hellfire.

She put on the containment jewellery and listened to Benny explaining the major problem with Freddy's kind of magic.

"Freddy is a mage by virtue of the energy from the demon zone that flows through her, but it isn't what you think. There is a pinhole in her soul, and the fire continues to pour out even if she doesn't use it. The hole isn't under her control, so the moment that she reaches critical, well, you saw it. She would have cried, vomited, and bled fire until she had expended it, but her body would have been healing her, so it would have taken days. The restrictors are a great idea, but they are dangerous without a pressure valve."

Symon nodded.

Freddy exhaled. "Sorry, I didn't think about it. I have always been called to use the power, so this is only the second time that it has happened. The first time, I was a teenager."

He waved his hand, and the wards around the shop opened. The presence of the XIA deterred the rush of the crowd that had formed.

Freddy chuckled. "Aw, we took their fun away."

Benny raised her phone and snapped a photo. "Not my fun. I just found my Christmas card photo."

Freddy looked down and groaned. "Come on. Be nice."

Tremble smiled, and he bowed low. "I never thought to see this side of you, Freddy."

"Why? Is my skirt tucked in my waistband or something?"

Argyle snorted. "He means you look pretty, Freddy."

She smirked. "Thank you. You all look very well, by the way. Positively glowing. Smith, are you pregnant?"

The agent recoiled. "Don't tease."

She cackled. It was always fun to play with Benny and her men.

A familiar face at the entry to the booth reminded her of the deal she had struck that morning.

"Darn. I will be back in a bit. I have to go dance."

Tremble perked up. "Dance?"

She scowled at him. "Right. Yes. Dance. Yesterday it was fun, today it is part of my job."

Benny grinned. "You know we are going to watch."

"I know. Symon, can you finish putting my jewellery on for me?"

He nodded and efficiently got her back to the appearance she had had a few minutes earlier. "There you go. All secure."

She nodded. "Excellent. See you in half an hour or so."

The female elf that was waiting for her passed her in the doorway and gave her a smack on the ass. "Go get 'em."

Freddy grinned and headed for the stage where the music wrapped around her and pulled her in. When Mosk held out his hand, she took it, and the rest was a wild blur of energy, laughter, and movement.

Chapter Ten

She had just finished the second set by sliding across the polished floor when she felt the first tug.

She excused herself and began walking toward Symon's booth when she felt a stabbing in her guts.

Benny was at her side in an instant. "What is it?"

Freddy gritted her teeth. "It feels like a summons, but it can't be. We cut the tie."

Benny held her up. "She is calling your blood. I can see it."

Freddy didn't know what that meant, but she knew that if it didn't stop soon, she was going to start screaming.

Argyle picked her up and carried her over to Symon's booth. Symon met them on the way.

"What is happening?"

Benny filled him in. "The bitch that she was tied to is pulling at her is my guess. The last time she was there, there was plenty of blood, and even an idiot can manage a blood call. We have to find her or shut down the link."

Symon wrapped his hands around Freddy's wrists, and she felt a pulse of power move across her skin. It connected at all the laced metal that she was wearing and spread over her head. The pain stopped, and she gasped.

Symon nodded to Argyle, and he shifted, handing Freddy over to her mage.

She was recovering from the pain and didn't orient herself until she was sitting in his workshop.

He set her down on his work stool,

and he gave her a quick check. "She shouldn't have been able to do that. Where did she get the blood?"

"She tried to kick me to death the last time I saw her. There was plenty of blood for her to choose from." Freddy's heartbeat was thudding in her chest.

"I have put a protective web around you, but I don't know how long I will be able to maintain it if we have any distance between us."

She sighed. "Right. So, do you want to come to my place, or shall I go to yours?"

"Right now, we are staying here. There is no way for your attacker to get into the Faire." He stroked the sweaty hair from her cheek.

"Ah, right. I should get back to work."

He shook his head. "Stay here. Rest for a few minutes. Your friends are waiting outside, so come out when you feel more like yourself."

Freddy watched him go, and she heard the voices of folks discussing what to do with her and how to handle her. Freddy stood up, shook her skirts out, and went to greet her nearest and dearest.

"I am not going to be handled. I will face her, and that will be the end of it."

Benny blinked. "You can do that?"

"Sure. She isn't my mage anymore, but I need her to challenge me." She looked to Symon. "I think I know how to do that, but I am going to need bait."

He stared at her. "Me?"

"Sure, if she can cut our tie, she has a chance to claim me again. She can file for a reassignment. She can't kill you, but she can maim you."

He scowled. "She would have a hard time doing that."

"She doesn't play fair. She uses concealed charms and throws them like hand grenades."

"I stand forewarned. She still isn't getting her hands on you." He touched her cheek and stroked her skin with his thumb.

She desperately wanted to lean into the touch, but this was war, for lack of a better term. She met his gaze and kept her expression soft. "Well, if I am here for the night, I had better get to work."

Benny sighed. "You are too stubborn for your own good."

"It is the demon zone leaking through." She wrinkled her nose.

Benny groaned. "Right. Of course. Well, we have seen your performance on the stage, so now, we have to return to work. Keep us posted as to your situation. I will text you near dawn."

Freddy hugged her. "Of course, buddy. Now, take your team and go fight crime, or wait for me to start a riot. Your choice."

Benny looked her in the eye, and she

winced. "Right. We are leaving. Come on, fellas."

Freddy stood with her bejewelled arms crossed and watched them go. When they had left the booth, she sighed in relief. "Whew. I thought I was going to have to strip naked on the main stage."

Symon stared. "You would have done it?"

"I don't make empty threats. She knows it."

"I see. Well, we have customers, so do what you do so well."

Freddy nodded. "Off I go, Mage Symon."

She sold an illusion of masculinity to a merman in the form of an arm cuff, earrings that would muffle sound to a werewolf with keen hearing, and a pair of large wedding rings were sold to a troll woman who was shopping for her son.

Each receipt was written up, record-ed, and the funds were processed before the item was handed over. There were two attempts at shoplifting, but Freddy wandered over and offered to hold the mirror while the vampire tried them on.

The vampire's companion was snick-ering, but Freddy merely asked if they wanted the companion piece to the bracelet they had just palmed.

Both items were returned to her, and the vampires left.

She worked through the night when the gong sounded. She smiled ruefully and shook her head. "Well, there goes that contract."

Symon came toward her, and he frowned. "What?"

"Mosk was supposed to have food de-livered to me. Nothing has shown up, so the deal is off."

He smiled. "Really?"

"Yes. I am depending on folk to keep

their word."

"Fair enough. Are you ready to shed your extra weight?"

She chuckled. "Yes, Symon. Take it off... take it all off."

He snorted and took her hand, guiding her back to the workshop. He removed her metal wear and placed it on dummies for safekeeping. When she was clear of the extra silver and jewels, he smiled. "If you want to change into your regular clothing, I will wait outside."

"Please." She smiled and kept that smile in place until he was out of her sight. Freddy could feel her face pulling into lines of pain. The ward that he had put on her had stopped the agony, but the muscles that had felt the abuse were still sore.

It took all her effort to remove her outfit and put on her underwear and sundress. The sandals were a delightful relief. She didn't think she could tie her own shoes at that point.

When she was texting Benny to let her know that she was going to Symon's place, she wandered out into the booth, and Symon nodded. "Wait here."

She looked around and took a mental inventory of the stock that was left in the booth. She heard a knocking at the door to the booth, but the shield had kicked in while she was changing. The dark figure at the edge of the booth was insistent, and it knocked again.

Freddy saw the outline of the body, and she froze. "How the hell did she get here?"

Symon walked out of the back in jeans and a tight shirt. "Who is here?"

"*She* is here."

"You are serious?"

"Yes."

"So, this is going to happen here."

"Apparently. Remember, try to get her to challenge me. I will do my own taunting."

He gave her a dark look, and he stepped toward the doorway with a determined stride. Freddy walked behind him, and when they passed through the doorway, the figure was gone. The flap of the cover fell across the shop opening, and their backs were covered.

Symon reached back and took her hand, leading her toward the open space of the stage.

There was a rustle of energy before the first fireball came toward them.

Freddy tackled Symon, and the projectile sailed over their heads.

The British voice said coldly, "Where is she?"

Symon got to his feet. "Who?"

"My familiar. The dog. Where is my damned dog?"

Freddy slowly got to her feet. "You don't have a familiar. The transfer was ratified by the Mage Guild, both here and in the UK."

"Bullshit. No one told me that. Where is she?"

Freddy scowled. "Standing right in front of you, asshole."

Martha stared. "No. My familiar is a dog."

"No, your familiar was under a curse administered by the guild. It is transferable, and now, you don't have one. Tada."

Symon came to stand next to her but slightly to the front. "I have volunteered to take her on, and now, she is my familiar."

"You can't have her. She is my familiar." Martha used her power move and blasted at Symon with all of her energy.

Symon was struck, and he staggered back. Freddy watched, and when he struck back with the metal and fire, she placed her hand on his shoulder. The demon fire mixed with his energy, and the bolt that struck Martha sent her back twenty feet, and when she landed, she was smoking.

They approached her, and she was moving slightly, but her body was so full of drugs and scorched tissue that it was doubtful she would get up again.

"Call the Mage Guild." Freddy whispered it softly.

A voice behind them spoke. "Unnecessary. So, this is the idiot?"

Freddy turned to see Hyl as he approached. "Yes, this is her."

"I have this. Go and get some rest, possibly a healing spell. You are damaged."

Freddy nodded and leaned against Symon. "I think we should go now."

Symon nodded and looked down at his hands. "What was that?"

"That was properly harnessed power from the demon zone. Come on. You can buy me breakfast again."

He smiled slightly. "You want to go for food after that?"

"Blasting the wicked makes me hungry."

He laughed and watched as Hyl casually flipped the scorched mage onto her belly before cuffing her hands behind her back.

"She will be held and charged with interference between a mage and familiar. Were there any other assaults?"

Freddy nodded. "I was under a blood attack earlier in the day."

"I will look into it. It is a serious charge, so I look forward to slapping her with it."

"I will put any memories into a display if necessary."

"I will make a note of that."

Hyl disappeared with his prey. A moment after he had spoken, the spot was empty.

Symon looked at her. "You still want

food?"

"I need to eat, and you said you would take care of me. I am holding you to it."

He cocked his head. "Really?"

"Yes, and the guild is going to need to see what happened, so it is easier if they can get us both at the same place. They tend to haul away the familiars first and torture them before questioning their mages." She wrinkled her nose.

"In that case, let's return to my home, and we will have something to eat and get some rest."

Freddy nodded. "Please. I am feeling a little vulnerable right now."

He smiled and offered her his arm. "I would be honoured for you to accompany me."

She wrapped her hand around his forearm, and they walked to the gate. Sure, there were witnesses to the event, but they gave the mages a wide berth. It was mage business, and the extranaturals stayed out of it.

Chapter Eleven

The snug Tudor-style home suited him. Freddy sat in the kitchen and watched as he made them each a cheese and mushroom omelette.

"How big is the property?" She smiled as he set the plate down in front of her.

"Five acres. I have my forge out back, but the rest is wild." Symon flipped his own omelette once and then slid it onto a plate.

Herbal tea took the place of coffee as they were going to try to get what rest they could.

"Do you have a garden?" Freddy's question was anything but casual.

"No. I bought this place five years

ago, and I have been going non-stop ever since. No time for landscaping or horticulture."

She nodded and took her first bite of the food. "Wow. This is good." Freddy said it as she was sucking air into her mouth. The omelette was also extremely hot.

He sat next to her. "It is my go-to when I am working. I am never more than five minutes from a hot meal."

She chuckled. "How much longer is the Faire running?"

"Only a week."

She nodded. "So, ideally, I would be there with you for the rest of the week."

"That is the plan. Why are you suddenly talking like you aren't going to be here?"

Freddy wrinkled her nose. "I have no idea what the guild is going to say. My ancestor was punished for fighting a legal duel against a bully, so I am not confident in their judgment."

"Ah. That. I will stand with you."

She smiled at him. "I know you will, but that doesn't really matter to them."

"When do you think they will call?"

Freddy snorted. "At the most inconvenient time."

Symon nodded. "That does sound like them."

She finished her meal and took her empty plate and his for a trip to the sink. She quickly washed them and set them on the draining board.

She turned and leaned back against the sink. "So, where am I sleeping?"

"I am not trying to be forward, but I can protect you more easily if you and I are in contact. So, with clothing on but my room?"

She nodded and let out a tremendous yawn. "I think that is fine."

He chuckled. "Right. This way."

He led her through his home and up

to a loft that overlooked a huge living room. Freddy kicked off her shoes and climbed into the bed, her eyes drifted shut before he had climbed in next to her. She felt him wrap an arm around her waist and spoon her, but the smile on her lips was the feeling of security that he was giving her.

Even an hour of sleep would be enough to wash away the stress of the day.

Someone was shaking her shoulder. "Freddy. They have come for us."

She nodded and sat up. The three guild officers surrounding the bed were not a surprise. Hyl's grinning face behind them was the surprise.

She scooted off the bed and put on her sandals. Symon put on his own shoes, and when he was ready, the guild officers surrounded them.

There was a surge of power, and when

the light faded, they were standing in the middle of a hall in the Mage Guild.

Symon moved to be next to Freddy and took her hand. She squeezed his roughly textured hand and looked at the tribunal that was lined up on a dais.

The guild officers urged them to approach the dais, so Freddy stepped forward and smiled brightly.

"Honour of the day to you, sirs and madam." Freddy bobbed a curtsy.

"Fredericka, cursed familiar of the Shokar clan. You stand accused of assaulting a mage."

She looked at them. "That account is incorrect."

The mages looked at each other, but there was contempt in the central mage's eyes.

"You didn't ask which mage we were referring to."

She smiled. "There has only been one mage who attacked me in the last two years. This one person used to be the mage I was attached to, and she assaulted my current mage, my intended mage. He defended himself, and I acted within my purview to assist him."

The mages blinked and recoiled slightly. "That was not the account we were given."

"Well, if it came from the so-called victim, she would have a self-interest to protect."

The three murmured to each other.

Freddy looked to Symon, but his brow was furrowed, and he was trying to speak. She whispered, "Don't bother. They won't let you talk until they want to hear you."

He pressed his lips together, and he nodded. She squeezed his hand without moving, and he smiled slightly.

The mages finished speaking to each other, and their spokesman turned to her. "The officers indicated that they found you in bed with your mage. Are you using your body to gain his agreement?"

Freddy shook her head. "Did your officers mention that we were both clothed and on top of the covers? I am dressed now as I was then."

The mage looked to the officers, and they nodded.

"Your previous mage has made grievous claims against you."

"I have no doubt. If I can be pressed to a truth orb, you can ask me whatever you like."

Symon was squeezing her hand, but she ignored him.

The mage raised his brows. "You want to be pressed to the truth?"

"I want this over and done. One day's pain may buy me the rest of my life. It is a risk I accept."

The mage trio nodded. "Done. Officers, summon an orb and bring in the plaintiff."

Hyl and one of the other officers summoned a truth orb that was nearly as tall as they were.

It took ten minutes, but Martha was escorted in, and her skin was healed and bright red. The expression on her face was smug. She loved causing trouble.

"Mage Martha Smith, we are here to hear your grievance against your former familiar, and something has come to light."

Martha frowned. She hated being questioned. "What?"

The mage blinked and then followed up. "It appears your description of events was not the only version. We are here to press the truth out of your former familiar, and she will answer what we ask."

Freddy nearly belted out a hoot of laughter. Martha had turned green.

She whispered to Symon. "Make sure

they ask about what she used me for. It is important."

He nodded.

"Fredericka, will you please enter the orb." The mage spokesman leaned forward.

She nodded and walked into the orb. Her hands and feet were pulled toward the edges, and the magic pressed in on her.

"Familiar, what are your recollections of last night? The altercation between your mage and your ex-mage?"

Freddy held still as the magic pressed in on her. She thought of the moment, and she felt it leave her body.

* * * *

Symon watched as Freddy's face barely contorted with what had to be an agonizing pressure. The memory emerged from her and floated up above the orb, playing back from the moment she saw the shadow at the door until she added her power to his to stop the other mage.

The council looked confused.

Symon raised his hand, and suddenly, he was free to speak. "Would it benefit you to learn why her ex-mage wanted her back so badly? What purpose she was fulfilling?"

The council nodded, and the central one asked, "Familiar, what did you do for your previous mage?"

Bubbles began to flow up hard and fast. Within the orb, Freddy was screaming as hundreds of images left her memories and were displayed above.

Images of animals fighting surrounded by cheering mages filled the bubbles. She bit, clawed, and was savaged in turn.

Symon looked toward Martha, and it was apparent that she had tried to exit the room. Two guards held her fast as they stared in horror.

When Freddy's hellhound body was used to attack another mage, that was enough for the council. They stopped the orb, and Freddy fell to her knees.

Symon helped her to her feet, and he kept an arm around her. She was coated in sweat, but her jaw was set. She was determined. He helped her stand straight.

The council looked at her. "Were you used in fights against standard animal familiars?"

Martha was actively struggling now.

Freddy nodded. "I was. I was a fight dog with an enchantment placed on me that made the other combatants' mages forget that they had ever seen me before. I would fight the same familiars over and over for Martha's profit."

The council leaned back and talked to each other for a moment before nodding, and the central mage looked at

Freddy with accusing eyes. "Why was this matter never brought to the Mage Guild's attention?"

Freddy straightened her shoulders. "I tried. On seventeen separate occasions, I petitioned the guild for a hearing, but I was denied under the assumption that I was petitioning for my freedom. All I wanted was a respectable mage, and now, I have one."

He looked at her. "How did that come about?"

"I was attending an event at Ritual Space which caused me to be unable to respond to her summons. When I was out of the constricted area, she summoned me and then attempted to kick my familiar form to death in front of witnesses. When I returned to my friends, they got me to a healer and provided me with these cuffs, which were wrought by Symon. They stopped me from being pulled to her until things could be corrected."

They looked at each other. "Do you have witnesses to your state?"

"Sure. Minerva is my friend and healer. She took care of me with her mate and sent me home when I was physically ready."

Symon knew that name. She was a tremendously powerful mage who was living in a distant city with a dragon.

"Minerva? The spell-maker?"

Freddy nodded. "The very same. I have known her for over a decade, and she is a very reliable witness, as is Beneficia Ganger. She has seen me bloody and torn more than once."

"So, your opinion is that you have been tortured."

Freddy cocked her head. "No, I am concerned that I was used to torture others. Aside from my connection to the demon zone, I am not a monster. The shape that I have to wear during an attack is one that has been forced on my bloodline. I hate that it was used to hurt anyone."

They paused to deliberate again. When he leaned forward again, he sounded tired. "Would you be willing to testify against your previous mage when we hold her tribunal?"

"Yes, but I will not undergo the orb again. You can use a writing book or other means. The images you have recorded today are sufficient for your purposes."

"Of course. Mage Symon Smith, do you have anything to add to these proceedings?"

Symon took a deep breath and inclined his head. "I believe that Freddy has said it all. She is a good woman, an excellent mage, and what has been done to her is horrendous. I am appalled that the guild has allowed it to continue as long as it has. She may be a familiar, but she is a mage first and entitled to as much representation as any of us."

The head of the council nodded. "We find the charges against Fredericka the familiar to be unfounded, and a motion for reparations will be entered to assess her family's continued penance. The mage Martha Smith will be held pending an investigation into misuse of a familiar and abuse of memory magic."

A gavel slammed down and light swirled. When Symon looked down at Freddy, she was grinning and crying.

Chapter Twelve

reddy leaned up and kissed Symon right on the lips. He paused for a moment and then wrapped his arms around her and returned the affection.

When she pulled back, he gave her a heavy-lidded look. "I am guessing that the arms-length situation is over?"

"I couldn't risk it, knowing that she was going to try and manipulate the system. If we had slept together and they knew it, it would have tainted our testimony in the eyes of the guild. They always think the worst of familiars."

Freddy noted that his hands were still around her waist. She leaned against him. "Once Martha has been sentenced, we can do whatever we want."

She pressed her forehead to his chest, and she could hear the thudding. "On the other side, I don't need to stay quite so close to you anymore."

He sighed. "Isn't there some other peril out there that you could get into so that you can stay with me?"

She grinned, keeping her head down. "I think I can manage something. I mean, I do have to help you with the Faire for the next week, right?"

He sighed, and his hands flexed against her back. "Yes. That isn't enough time, but I suppose that I could ask you out on a proper date after that."

Freddy's heart lifted. "Yes, you could do that. Or I could ask you."

Symon chuckled. "There is that."

She heard a chime and looked around. "What time is it?"

"It isn't past noon. We have plenty of time."

She saw her phone and the flashing light. "Damn. I forgot about Benny."

She ducked away from Symon's embrace and picked up her phone. The texts scrolling by in a heavy cascade spoke to Benny's agitation.

Why is the guild calling me about your returning from your summons banged up?

Where are you?

OMG, what the hell happened?

Are you okay?

Is Symon okay?

Why aren't you answering?

I am coming over there.

Wait, I am at your place. Where are you?

Shit. I am heading to Symon's.

Freddy checked the time of the last text, and she winced. "Sorry, Symon. Brace for invasion by the XIA."

"They are coming?"

Freddy heard the thud of vehicle

doors. "They are here."

She headed down the stairway that attached to the loft, and Symon followed her.

The quartet in black came through the door, and Benny rushed at her, hugging her tight. "I got a briefing from Hyl. What the hell?"

"She is in custody, and she isn't able to cast her memory spell, so she will have to admit to some of her activities."

Symon took the men into the other room, so Freddy sat down with Benny and explained the activities of the evening and morning.

* * * *

Symon served iced tea to the three agents, and they sipped it and looked him over. The elf asked him, "What are your intentions toward our Freddy?"

Symon blinked and looked at them

all. Each was looking at him with the glare of an older brother.

"My intentions are to help her to be happy and then maintain that state. She is learning how to live again, and it will be delightful to be at her side while she does it."

The elf leaned forward. "What if you are not what she wants?"

Symon blinked. He hadn't considered that. "I suppose I would have to encourage her to seek out whomever it is that makes her happy, even if it isn't me."

The shifter cocked his head and then grinned. "Good answer. Make sure that you do what you can, and she will put her own weight in the relationship. Freddy may be light-hearted, but she is also a good soul. That goodness can get her into trouble, but if you need help defending her, feel free to call."

The vampire snorted. "Call Benny. She isn't great at transporting, but she will have us here in minutes."

Symon chuckled. "I will."

They fell into silence, and he still felt the judgment that was washing over him. When the elf leaned in and asked, "How much do you make?" Symon was on familiar ground. Finally.

He explained his financial situation, and the men nodded in approval.

The elf murmured, "Benny's birthday is coming up. Could you make something for her?"

Symon went to a drawer on one side of the kitchen island and pulled out a pencil and paper. "What would you like and what kind of enchantment?"

They gathered around and discussed what they thought they should give to their partner, and Symon waited patiently until they were done debating. Freddy and Benny were laughing and chatting in the front room, and it was a lovely sound.

They had six hours before they had to be at the Faire, so that was plenty of time to get the XIA to make up their minds.

* * * *

Freddy swirled on the stage in Mosk's arms. He lifted her, and she bent, twisted, and twirled using her grip on his arm as her balance point.

The crimson and silver skirt swirled outward, and the costume added to the drama of the dance. When the pipes and strings wound to a quiet murmur, she settled on her feet, with her back to Mosk.

His apology for the night before had been sincere and accompanied by a new pair of boots and a cloak. Today, the moment she left the stage, the page would be dispatched to get her some food. Yesterday, the young male had gotten distracted by the object of his desire. Today, they were using a different and less horny page.

The applause was deafening, and she curtsied to Mosk before leaving the stage.

Familiar faces in the crowd got her attention. Imara and Argus were there, with her small kitten riding high on her shoulder.

"Good evening, Imara, Argus, Mr. E." Freddy bowed to all of them.

"Freddy, you look fantastic. I have been hearing that things have been exciting, and I am glad to see that your soul is brighter."

Freddy looked at Imara, and the young woman smiled slowly. If there was anyone who knew what a soul looked like, it was the Death Keeper and Master Mage. "Thanks for letting me know. It is good to have corroboration."

"Not a problem. I call them like I see

them." Imara winked.

"So, are you two out on a date?"

Argus grinned. "Yes. Finally. I have the night off, so we decided to check in on you. Mr. E was worried."

Freddy reached out and softly stroked the familiar. "Thanks for your concern. I am fine now, and I think I might be getting better."

I am glad. The mage you had was a psycho, and I know whereof I speak.

Freddy nodded and replied just as silently. *They are examining her behaviour, knowing that memory was manipulated, they will be able to launch an investigation.*

Good. I think she would benefit from a few decades as a familiar. The kitten letting out a sinister, hissing laugh made Freddy grin as wide as her mouth could manage.

She had to admit that Martha as a familiar was an excellent thought.

"I am heading back to the jeweller's booth. You are welcome to come with me."

Imara grinned. "I think I will leave you to it. We just arrived, and I still want to go exploring. This place is just too fun."

Argus grinned. "I will have to see if we can find the same tailor that you use. The outfit is great."

Freddy wrinkled her nose. "It can get a little drafty when I spin. But thanks."

She waved at the trio and headed for the booth. There was a woman in there who was walking around with a frown on her face.

Freddy knew her from somewhere, but she couldn't place her. "Can I help you?"

The woman nodded. "I am looking for a pendant, bracelet, or earrings that can be enchanted to hold a memory spell."

Freddy nodded and dismissed the elf

that had been admiring herself in the mirror.

"This way. How large do you want the pendant?"

The woman smiled. "I need two. I need one large and one as small as can be made."

"Just a moment. I will ask the artisan."

The woman nodded. "I will wait."

Freddy went to the forge where Symon was working on one of the custom orders from the first day.

"Symon?"

He kept his gaze on the metal between his hands. "Yes, Freddy?"

"I have a client who needs two pendants. Both need to be able to be enchanted for memory spells, but one has to be big and one tiny."

He paused his work and turned to her. "I can do it."

Freddy nodded. "Good. I get the feeling that it is urgent."

"Tell her to come back in two hours."

Freddy grinned.

She returned to the front of the shop, and a buffet of meats, cheeses, fruit, and meat pies were on a board with flagons of beverages. Mosk had come through.

The woman with chalky skin and dark hair was standing with a slight smile on her lips. "Two young women delivered it."

"It is my price to dance with one of the elves on the main stage." Freddy turned to her. "If you can return in two hours, the pendants will be ready."

The woman smiled. "Excellent. I will be back in two hours."

Freddy was going to offer the woman part of the feast, but she was gone in seconds. She thought about the client and tried to remember details, but they slipped away. She remembered dark hair and pale skin as well as huge eyes.

Freddy had felt the effects of a memory spell before, but this was different. It was as if the very air around her was trying to hide this woman from sight.

She gathered some food and brought it to Symon, and then, she returned and started grazing, stopping only to attend to shoppers.

Time spun past, Imara and her fellas came by for a short visit and to show off a fancy new cloak that Imara could wear on Death Keeper jobs. When the dawn gong was only a few minutes away, the mystery client returned.

"Are they ready?"

Freddy produced the two items, each on fine chains.

The woman handed over a large sheaf of cash. "Here. Take it."

Freddy took the money and counted off what she needed. When she looked up, the woman was gone.

The gong sounded, and she walked

over toward the forge while Symon was coming out. He saw the cash in her hand. "What is that?"

"She shoved the money at me and disappeared."

Symon looked at the bills. "Did you see this?"

She looked, and small words were printed along every edge. *Remember Me.*

There was something very sad about that woman, and Freddy was going to make every effort to remember her and her... dark hair?

Epilogue

*P*acking up the booth had been sad, but going back to Symon's where the entire cast of the Faire came over for a *Perpetual Night* barbeque was fascinating.

Freddy was sitting and laughing with some of the dancers when an imposing figure arrived at the party.

Hyl was standing there in all of his black and threatening glory. The basket of fruit on his arm was incongruous.

"Hyl, what are you doing here?"

He smiled. "Adrea wished you to have a portion of your first harvest. It is a slow start, but your trees are bearing fruit twisted together."

Symon came out of the conversational group that he had been in. "Really?"

Freddy grinned.

Hyl snorted. "They bloomed and fruited two days ago. There is no question why. Just take your little sex apples, and I will be on my way."

Freddy was laughing, and she walked up to him and hugged him. "Adrea is a lucky lady."

"She knows it." He winked at her and shoved the basket at her. "I would not recommend eating these in a public forum."

Symon took the apples, and Freddy linked arms with him. "I will keep these in a safe place."

Freddy laughed as he left her and went to the house to put the apples somewhere that folks wouldn't get a hold of them.

Freddy returned to her conversational partners. She tried to pay attention, but her mind crept back to Ritual Space.

When Symon returned, she looked at him as he heckled Hector at the barbeque. What kind of fruit would be produced by the tree of fire and metal?

It was going to be a while before they found out, but that would mean a trip to Ritual Space. There was no way that whatever came out of there was going to be safe to hand around.

* * * *

The barbeque turned into an orgy when someone got into the apples and handed them around.

Freddy couldn't stop anyone, so she just headed up to the roof and kept the shadows lit with balls of fire from the demon zone. Now that Symon had put release valves into the links, she was free to vent her energy when she needed or wanted to. For the first time in her life, she was as free as a familiar could be.

The rest of her life was looming in front of her and fear was no longer part of the equation. She chuckled and let another orb of fire float down across the yard. Altering her behaviour to reflect her newfound security was going to take a lot of energy, but Symon was willing to hold her hand and help her out. He knew when to help and when to keep his ideas to himself, and that knowledge made him an easy person to love.

Her fire flared as she realized what she had just admitted to herself. She glanced over at him where he was sitting with a sketchpad and drawing a picture of her. Yeah, it was love. She didn't care who would say it first; it was going to last until both of their fires went out.

Apologies for the delay. In January this year, my siblings and I purchased a plot of land, and when we got into it in mid-April, we got to work. We have put in a garden (planters), an orchard (deer got at it), and made a bee yard.

That's right, we are now beekeepers, and we have a YouTube channel and an Instagram. Mystery Bees Apiary. Yes, it is named after the infamous kitten, Mr. E.

So, now that we are on summer maintenance, I hope to be able to work a proper schedule with my writing once again. If you want to know what I am doing... check YouTube. We are putting up beekeeping videos every few days.

Thanks for reading,

Viola Grace

About the Author

Viola Grace (aka Zenina Masters) is a Canadian sci-fi/paranormal romance writer with ambitions to keep writing for the rest of her life. She specializes in short stories because the thrill of discovery, of all those firsts, is what keeps her writing.

An artist who enjoys a story that catches you up, whirls you around and sets you down with a smile on your face is all she endeavours to be. She prefers to leave the drama to those who are better suited to it, she always goes for the cheap laugh.

www.ingramcontent.com/pod-product-compliance
Lightning Source LLC
Chambersburg PA
CBHW070506200726
48293CB00007B/2408